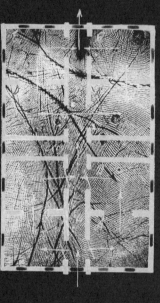

D1607622

hymns to millionaires

HYMNS TO MILLIONAIRES • SOREN A. GAUGER

twisted spoon press · prague · 2004

For Scotia

ISBN 80-86264-18-1

contents

HOW I GOT RID OF IT

"This is my dog," said these poor children. "That is my place in the sun." There is the origin and image of universal usurpation. (295)

Pascal, "Wretchedness"

It would not be untoward of me to describe the little scene taking place around me at this very moment. I am riding my usual tram to the small office where I daily confront the patients who gather every morning and seep from one room to the next like a suppurating sore ... I am midway between home and office, a point where the tram encounters a bridge of considerable length and crosses it. A brick has been thrown through a window of the car I am riding in, causing the other passengers to erupt into a state of pandemonium. Taking advantage of this fortuitous disorder, I heave up the large and cumbersome box that has been resting at my feet and push it out of the window above my head. I then hurriedly reseat myself and adopt a calm expression, all the while listening intently for the kerplop that will signify the sinking of the box in the river flowing beneath the bridge. I do not hear the sound, yet dare not swivel my head. A pear-shaped gentleman delivers me a glancing blow to the occiput with his elbow. He is so devoured by the pedestrian conundrum of the brick that he has begun bellowing about the safety-risk facing his two toad-like infants and, clearly suffering from some form of psycho-histrionic disorder, frequently observed in overweight men of his age group, is flapping his arms about in a visual demonstration of his anxiety syndrome. A gentleman with pattern hair loss struggles to pacify him. A woman says something about the rising price of bread. I return to my thoughts. There has been no kerplop.

A large puddle awaits my foot as I step off the tram, but with a deft maneuver I manage to evade it. This evasion brings me into headlong collision with Ms. Colleen Moore. I feel the stiffened muscles in my face involuntarily soften. Our gazes connect for a fleeting moment, and she purses her lips ever so slightly before boarding the tram, leaving me in her vast wake. I collect myself and head for the office, my very first step lunging me into the waiting humiliation of that self-same puddle.

The staircase to my office is irregularly steep and narrow. The architect was a clear-cut case of Childhood Deprivation Disorder; if only I had been given six weeks with him I'm sure I wouldn't have patients snapping their frail joints on those treacherous stairs. By the time I wheeze up to my front door Mr. DeMire is already waiting for me, unconsciously tap-tap-tapping away with his right foot, the poor devil. Fumbling for the keys, I recall to mind — my memory no doubt aided by the invincible metronome of DeMire's leather sole — how that very same sound drove his wife to suicide, the sheer melodrama of a fifth-story window, no less, and how his tapping now had a double-entendre effect that might move the stoniest of hearts to sorrow. With a decisive and swift movement I bring my foot heavily down upon his, and the sound abruptly quits.

We shuffle together through the waiting room and into my office, the two being divided by a glass door that slides rather than swings. This brings us to a further architectural eccentricity: my perfectly circular office. At precisely the center point stands my great oak desk and double-padded chair where I place myself each day. Somewhere in front of that one finds the client's chair. A cursory inspection would lead one to conclude that it is not a seat of privilege. The seat is worn, its sober shade of maroon faded, the legs scratched up from decades of anxious picking and fiddling.

If I were to superimpose, one on top of another, all of my clients from the past twenty-four years, all sitting at once on that unmoored satellite just slightly outside of arm's reach (I command a rather considerable arm-span), would it be any surprise to find them all blur into their one harmonious chord, an all-consuming wretched grimace, a disfigured Cheshire Cat? Onto this seething morass hops Mr. DeMire, or rather the thirty-ninth installment of more or less the same DeMire. He blushes, stammers, scrapes at his teeth with a fingernail, overwinds his watch. I know his every gesture down to the smallest revolting peculiarity. When he visits my closet-sized washroom, he leaves spots of blood in the sink. Go on, I say, from where you left off on Tuesday. Despite my most earnest efforts my voice sounds flat and defeated. There had been no kerplop.

After the fire I guess I felt strangely calm. That came after my wife's suicide of course and my son's, erm, ardent, erm, dismissal of my role if I can put it in terms such as . . . well then my co-workers had already signed the petition to have me . . . what is the term . . . dismissed, well and what is a man after all, Doctor, if not his family and his profession and his home? What could I even start talking about that wouldn't make . . . well, I still met Claude for lunch and we could speak in French which might not seem to you like something, Doctor, but after all.

It has not always been like this. Before I opened a practice I had various consultations with my conscience, more than the occasional misgiving. Did I really want to hold myself accountable for the most miserable refuse of the social system? Naturally, no. Yet here I was, milling about in the meantime between idle jobs, complaining to anyone who would listen that I was a trained and qualified psychoanalyst. A mender of strayed and punctured souls, I would wax lyrical. And above all, I had to do something.

But I was terrified I would lose something of myself amongst the assembly of madmen that would become my daily company, to say nothing of my bread and butter, and even more of the transformation of my own psyche that becoming a psychoanalyst would entail. I dreaded the moment when the placid and velvety texture of the analyst's voice would defrost and slowly seep into my own, until requesting a bus ticket and urging Mr. DeMire to tell me about his son (once again) would be one and the same smooth modulation.

My son . . . my son never wonders about me, I guess he doesn't wonder about things generally, oh, I'm well past the point where I can be counted upon to tread lightly about the topic of my son one can't go on being charitable for all one's life after all . . . He called me last week to tell me about his new job as a photographer's assistant and I said that's perfect for someone so duplicitous and then there was a long pause such as I'm accustomed to having when on the phone with my son and we, erm, mutually agreed to end the conversation. I have had nightmares since about the whole thing . . . Do you like hearing people's dreams, Doctor?

I nod my head and remember, as I always do when I nod my head, the first scrap of paper I wrote on and filed away, simply: "A nod of the head is either a gesture of agreement or an admission of guilt, or the last, helpless movement before the blackness of sleep." Why do I mention this . . . Ah, yes, because it marked the debut of what was to become a twenty-three-and-a-half year succession of little notes farmed from the steadily eroding treasuries of my innermost psyche as it once was and yet may be again. My theory ran like this: a personality can only be said to exist insofar as it has an outlet, much like a kind and virtuous God can only be said to exist if, amongst the petty tyrants and mercenaries praying to their gods of punishment and retribution there exists a solitary prayer (even one will do) to sweet Mercy. My notes were emphatically not, therefore, symbolic gestures, but rather fragments of a meek and huddled reality, shivering in the chill draft of the analyst's comforting smile. A little bell clangs in the back of my mind. How does it feel.

Well, I'm less, erm, vulnerable, if I have the right expression, to the nocturnal attacks of anxiety that simply . . . seep through the body, as well as what I call the falling sickness and a general brittleness in the fingers and teeth. But then something will confront me suddenly and without warning, the hernia and flash of a light bulb when I haven't any spares in the cupboard or the insufferable drip of a faucet, even when plugged up tight with toilet paper, the resolute tap-tap-tap

, he mimicked, providing unconscious syncopation to the rhythm of his eternally restless foot. I vow to myself to carpet the spot of floor under the patient's chair prior to DeMire's next visit. Meanwhile, the off-kilter rhythm has reminded me of a jazz melody popular some ten years ago, and I am helplessly thrust back to the Indian-red interior of an acquaintance's apartment, where the song in question is playing in the background and skipping strategically in order to delete the verses I have forgotten. The women's skirts ride just above the knee, in accordance with the fashion then, and their hair-configurations tower and spiral madly up from their foreheads, as though to foreshadow the Babel-like confusion that would descend upon me when I approached one of them sweatily clutching some elaborate cocktail. I was on my own and therefore I thought it prudent to strike up some of the old conversation. After a survey of the premises had occupied me for an hour or so, my gaze alighted upon a svelte woman in an evening dress, also on her own. Her slender, bare arms were propped up nonchalantly on a ledge behind her, and I don't think I will ever see anything more lovely than those arms, like swan necks reeling back in the mythic, righteous act of taking. My knees, suddenly the arbitrarily-chosen center of gravity, launched me forward, and from halfway across the room she happened to catch my eye. I noticed her full lips pucker ever so slightly. I hesitated, swooning, as if struck by a trance, which provided just enough time for a swarthy Mediterranean-type in a tan suit and shiny shoes to writhe in-between us, thrusting forward a hairy palm to shake and offering ejaculations of greeting to the disarmed target. Thus it was from afar that I first heard her sigh out her name: Colleen Moore.

. . . interesting than staying at the shelter for arson victims or listening to Claude complain about the stiffness in his legs, which . . . erm . . . he presumes to be, well, a signal or more of an omen, really, of a general stiffening of the joints and . . . well, a general paralysis, which is just another way of saying death, isn't it. So Claude's been in bad spirits and there can be nothing more depressing than a gloomy Frenchman do you know what I'm saying.

From that time forward my notes became more and more preoccupied with that phantom woman, who I am calling Ms. Colleen Moore. At least everything started with Ms. Moore, as if she were a center point from which my otherwise barren thoughts would drift in steady elliptical orbits, always to swing back to the same invariable with a magnetic irresistibility, a seemingly counter-geometrical veer towards the heart of the matter, that is to say . . . it should be abundantly clear at this juncture that I was losing control of the central control mechanism . . . that is, I now had three competing parties inside myself: the psychoanalyst, the self that kept seeing a certain woman's face in his periphery and writing absurd drivel that she would never lay her eyes upon, and the final self that could only stare at the whole grotesque bagatelle in abject horror. For years I juggled this trinity! It may be true that a man can persuade himself to endure any atrocity, no matter how appalling, if he finds a germ of necessity in it. I suppose this is where my dog starts to come in.

Come in, she cried, and so when I opened that doom-laden door which I firmly believe I was bound to open and which in a certain sense I have been perpetually reopening like some kind of brain-damaged Sisyphus every day for the past five years, when I opened that door there was my wife naked and clutching her belly in laughter and what's more the spotty backside of some flabby Casanova in an act of prostration to some god that was surely covering his eyes to avoid seeing our mutual triptych of humiliation: the physical, the circumstantial, and mine, the cumulative. And then what was there to do but to close the door and walk off.

My dog was born in the wrong skin. A monstrous semblance of a creature that whelped at the slightest injury to a paw. I have wondered if perhaps my apartment had had a floor-length mirror, if the beast would have seen its own terror-inspiring form and made the abstract leap of faith that it was one and the same as the reflection . . . but these are mad hypotheses. I bring up my dog because one fine day, having been pushed to the very limits of revulsion with myself . . . or, if I may clarify, with the periodic notes I had been writing and storing in the desk drawer . . . I solemnly resolved to be finished with the entire business once and for all. This was how I began . . . erm, well . . . — I suppose I began to snip up the notes into pieces, mixing the bits with the dog's dinner, and then feeding it all to him. The process was a slow one, because the dog would refuse to eat more than a certain percentage of paper as compared to meat, but then I thought a slowness to be appropriate . . . even necessary . . . to the act I was performing. Why, to throw it all in a hastily prepared fireplace would have been . . .

. . . an attic, filled with deflated balloons and vague whispers and indistinct outlines of furniture the floorboards creaking and tilting from side to side like the deck of a ship aware of a terrible parchedness in my throat and the knowledge that any attempt to speak would emerge as a dry croak towering piles of gray rubble imminent blindness a foregone conclusion rain incessantly tapping on the roof with impossible rhythm and is it any better to wake up

When the dog had devoured it all, our relationship began to change. He began looking at me with a smile that betrayed a strange wisdom, that spoke of a figurative digestion of the materials he had swallowed. Those eyes seemed to follow me wherever I was in the room, profoundly sad eyes, eyes that reached inside the marshy, malleable muck of my soul and pulled out the seeds, which I, imagine, I, was therefore confronted with in all their shriveled indignity. A dog!

I began the practice of locking him in the kitchen, until his sniveling howling got to be too much to bear. I stopped taking him out for walks during the day, out of fear that the passers-by would have even a tiny glimpse of what I saw in his condemning eyes. In short, I had not destroyed the papers at all, I had merely given them a new form, granted them an unspeakable autonomy, a new life, which was after all my life, and the dog's life, none of which I could control. Above all, I vowed not to do anything rash.

. . . spreading all over the shoulders and upper arms like a fire blazing out of control or an endless network of puddles of blood when I'm wide awake or dreaming or dreaming that I'm wide awake which all amounts to the same thing come to think of it . . .

And so there I was, shirt-sleeves rolled up and up to my elbows in blood, which I had painstakingly drained from the dog into an orange plastic bucket that I normally keep under the sink to catch the water that has leaked from a pipe since the very first day I moved into my apartment, a leak I have come to see as a necessary condition of life. The disposal of the blood was a simple enough matter, it just went down the bathtub drain. But the body of the dog was to prove more complex. I first cut it into pieces with a serrated blade, and wrapped each of the bits in plastic, twice over, so as to be sure, and then placed it all in a brown cardboard box.

But then how to get rid of the box.

Gradually, the transparent and flaky shards of a plan assembled themselves on the drafting table of my mind. I would take the box aboard the 8:10 tram, the one I normally take to work (nothing suspicious in that . . . all kinds of people take boxes onto trams for a multitude of reasons), and hire a man to cast a brick through the window as it was precisely reaching the midpoint of the bridge. I would take advantage of the ensuing mayhem, and unnoticed, heave the box out the window. Which leaves us only the affair of the kerplop, or rather the uncanny silence substituting for the anticipated kerplop. A silence that the wretched DeMire, my blood-sucking client, was parroting as he cradled his head in his big hands. With an impatient wave of the hand I sent him out of the room.

I remained in my office until nightfall, shifting papers from this pile to that, trying to calm the twitching of my hands. Then I made my way out to the street with a perfect air of tranquility. I mimed considering taking the tram home but then, with a shrug of the shoulders that would have been sure to convince any chance observers of my carefree motives, elected to walk home instead.

At the center of the bridge I stopped, as though struck by noticing the moon for the first time. Indeed, the shimmering lunar reflection on the surface of the water was not without its peculiar beauty. And as my gaze fell towards the river, I saw the box. It had fallen onto a ledge and was balanced precariously over the river's swiftly-running waters. All I would need to do was to swing a leg over the guardrail, give the thing a sure kick, and I would have no more of its torments. I glanced over my shoulder to be sure that the bridge was free of pedestrians.

I have often asked myself since, what if Ms. Colleen Moore hadn't stepped out of the mist at that moment. This belongs to the species of question that one asks oneself in the dead of night merely to feel the strange ecstasy of a chill run down one's spine. But the fact is that it was Ms. Colleen Moore, who had also chosen to walk home over the bridge on that enchanted evening. I lifted my gaze from the box and returned to my contemplation of the moon and its reflection. I heard her footsteps slow down as they approached, then falter and altogether stop. I swiveled to find her less than a few feet away, and smiling reassuringly at me. For an instant my instinct was to ignore her, I had the urgent matter of the box to be thinking about, not a second to waste, but then it hit me: wasn't it her in the box? And the dog? And I? And after all, weren't she and I in fact standing there on the pavement, intact?

We exchanged a few words, our breaths visible in the crisp night air, and then I found myself suggesting that we go for a stroll, which took us off the bridge, down the street, and in the direction of the moon.

THE JULIETTE VARIATIONS

But instead of that, I just grabbed Juliette firmly by the wrist, which to tell the truth seemed oddly willowy, I mean to say, fragile, in the bulk of my hand, I took her by the wrist and started dragging her off the fairgrounds. It may sound peculiar but everywhere I looked there was a fat man in a checkered suit leering purposefully at us, but that might have more to do with the state of my nerves than whatever was going on in, well, you know. Juliette had a thoughtful expression on her face. Well, what is it I said. My shoulder bag she said absently I think I've

The scraping of some carnival canzonetta censored the finish of her sentence. I pulled on that spindly wrist of hers again and got her to the relative calm of the stalls where heavyset men were aiming toy rifles at plastic ducks, saying damn the noise in this place. I think I have left my shoulder bag somewhere, probably said Juliette wiping her nose in the toilet (ping, ping, ping, ricochetting all around us). Juliette was born in Europe and still had the foul habit of calling a washroom a toilet which made me wince inwardly. Well then I muttered with a rising feeling of dread we'd better have a look. Juliette moved through the crowds as though pulled by an invisible Ariadne and it was all I could do to keep an eye on that undulating bun of hair submerging and then reappearing like a frolicsome porpoise a few arms' reaches ahead. I kept up for a few minutes but then from the corner of my eye I saw what looked like a beheading taking place on a stage to my left. I turned around abruptly but it proved to be only a device used for gauging one's strength by means of a mallet and a machine like an enormous thermometer. It was encircled by young men whose wolfish grins exposed rows and rows of sturdy teeth masticating bread and meat. I shuddered at the scene, my mind traveling through a gray parade of free associations, coffee mill to tourniquet to mousetrap I reached in front of me to clutch onto the wrist but I grabbed only air. Turning back in an attempt to spot Juliette's bun I saw only the backs of one hundred fat men in checkered suits and letting out a whimper of horror I started running towards the food area.

As might be imagined the food area was a strategically bad decision. Man eating is man at his most misshapen and grotesque man the pointless assembly of ligaments fatty tissues and gelatinous organs bundled up in a swath of rubbery skin. But surely the toi . . . washrooms were nearby that much could be counted on. I made up my mind to ask a waitress.

If only there had been one about. My attention wandered from a great luminous game board levitating in mid-air above the diners to the tables with their screaming children hopping about the furniture like contagious infections the puddles of spilled ketchup and squished French fries. To my immediate right sat an overweight gentleman with an orbicular nose engaged in the laborious consumption of large pieces of meat. The chewing sounds he made reached my ears with uncommon clarity the slurping of saliva the clicking of the jaws the juices of the meat savoringly sucked the little gagging noises at the back of the throat the elaborate finale of the swallow. I steeled my nerve. Have you seen a waitress I stammered my voice quavering. The man continued chewing although more contemplatively. I waited a minute and then said again with more of a note of urgency in the voice have you seen a waitress sir. The man pointed a corpulent finger at his lips and muttered can't you see I'm chewing. At the fairgrounds they always answer your questions with a question. Well yes sir I can

I said fairly choking on my oversized tongue I can see that you're chewing. At my house continued the fat diner his mouth full of half-chewed pork when a man's eating that's his chance for a little private time his time for reflection and deep consideration of the day's happenings and nobody but nobody feels at liberty to jostle him out of that. The father sits himself at the head of the table and raises a fork in his right hand he recited while demonstrating with his own plastic fork and after that the family knows the time for talking is through and it'll be only the content harmony of jaws workin' for the next twenty minutes or more. It's all finished when the father puts down his fork onto the plate and you hear that clink and again the fat diner tried to demonstrate and frowned at the failure of the plastic fork and plate to clink. Meanwhile the lumpiness of his cheeks had reminded me of the incident that had taken place not half an hour ago. I was with Juliette on the merry-go-round which was the only ride her delicate stomach would permit us and we had compromised on the gray horse (I had wanted a fiery black mare, Juliette some limpid white specimen) and seated ourselves upon it only a moment before the thing thrust forward with a mechanical lurch causing Juliette to half fall off. She laughed because the situation had its comic side but there was a fanged shadow of fear beneath it as I couldn't pull her all the way back onto the gray horse and she was left in the absurd predicament of dangling half-on and half-off with me holding on to her left calf for all I was worth. Which was fine at first but then it seemed that the merry-go-round was collecting speed and soon it was causing the children to holler

In scene two we are standing behind the scenes that is to say amongst the leviathan garbage bins while Juliette tries to coax her prudish throat into vomiting. It had been a fearful ride after all. I started wandering off to give her a bit of peace and also because she hates the smell of my cigarettes when of all people who should step out from behind a wall of garbage bins but this fat man in a checkered suit halfway to balding bolero and over-polished brogues. I took out a little box of wooden matches and with my spidery index finger pushed out the miniature drawer to reveal a nursery of eleven match heads and then to my surprise the fat man in the checkered suit was practically breathing down my neck I mean he was right on top of me. I lit myself a cigarette. That smile of his was positively sinister. Our proximity was making me anxious but he wasn't doing anything so I had nothing to react to. The worst part was that he reminded me precisely of my dead uncle Moe yes he was Moe all right down to the suspenders down to the slovenly way he pared his fingernails down to the cream-soupiness of his convex eyes. Uncle Moe was a man who tormented us all with the fact of his company laughed when I hurt myself and when I call to mind Uncle Moe it is in his workshop surrounded by long hanging bodies at that uncomfortable intermediate stage of no longer quite animal and not yet meat and I swear to you that smell haunts me still. This man wasn't Uncle Moe whose body wasn't recovered by the police until five days later incidentally he was his own corporal entity all right but the Uncle-Moeness in his every gesture had my nerves atingle from the start. He studied the way I lit my cigarette and pseudo-nonchalantly breathed in a bit of smoke and then said I'm surprised you have left her alone. Sorry I mumbled absently that girl with the straight brown hair he quickly clarified which was odd enough for me to look him in the eye which seemed to be free-floating unhooked from its moorings. It was Juliette the girl with the straight brown hair. What the hell do you mean by telling me that I blurted as he held up the palm of a hand to test if it had started to rain (it had: little pearls of rainwater were slipping into the finely-wrought canals in his palm). His reply was to flash me his macabre grin which he then concealed so instantly under a poker face that I was to doubt the efficacy of my own senses i.e. did the smile ever exist at all before turning on his heel and making silently off.

Landscape with bewildered, smoking man and garbage containers.

Wherein I moved with a grave immediacy to the spot where I remembered depositing Juliette whose face was strangely colorless when I at last saw it. She claimed she had staggered off to the toilet and when she came out there was this obese checker-suited . . . but what's the matter she crooned presumably I had blanched like a boiled almond.

Well and then we were off! Wrist crowd bun beheading wolves jaws snap-snap fat men food-area and then . . .

I'll tell you a thing or two chum about why the family's in such a sorry state know what I'm saying. It is because the sacrosanct zone of the supper table father children salt and pepper mother cutlery what have you is being sold for a song.

He paused here and in fact "Pop Goes the Weasel" was shimmering, was echoing through the length of the food pavilion. The pause allowed me to focus on why I was listening to this man sermonize on his two-penny dinner-table philosophy anyway. With the flat of my open palm I brusquely pushed the fat diner's nose so that he toppled over backwards in his chair cursing loudly. Everyone swiveled to have a good look. The diner resembled to no small degree an overturned turtle and the combined chaos of the place compelled me to look for the washrooms on my own waitress or no. I looked up again and there were those blinking lights constellations forming numbers I imagined were part of some great bingo game and what if the numbers continued to grow higher and higher until all of those playing stopped in mute awe and something was reached that wasn't just another number but something hit my jaw likely a fist and I went swooping to the floor.

I woke up and thanks to the blood my ear was stuck to the floor. The setting had changed a third time I mean it was the same dingy food court but the lights had dimmed the numbers had stopped their twinkling there was the sound of a broom in some remote corner sweeping up broken glass and the pale glow of a piece of the moon visible through the window. All the people had gone home for the night except that fat man in the checkered suit who was standing just over me and lighting himself a cigarette. My heart unused to such exertions as the day had shown gave an audible groan of anticipation as this new trauma caused it to thrash about in my chest like a fish thrown into a boat. It was no picnic I tell you. I lifted my ear off the ground and it made a sound like a cork coming out of a bottle of wine and with difficulty I tottered to my feet brushing the food bits off of my pants and noting with annoyance that I had been lying in a puddle of cola. When he spoke it wasn't to me, it was an address to the cosmos hurling abuse casting scorn shaking his fist reddening in the face dabbing the sides of his face with an enormous cotton-candy colored handkerchief. Then he cut himself off in mid-sentence as though something had just occurred to him and he looked as though he were about to sob. Pardon me I said but have you seen my friend and noticing the numbed expression on his face I clarified with the straight brown hair. His features thawed and he ran his great hands through his sweat-soaked hair causing it to stand up on end saying in a hushed voice by the time I arrived at the Ferris wheel there was nothing anyone could possibly do.

Of course, when I think of Juliette . . . when I think of Juliette I know that these are hopeless falsehoods. I know that I received a small white envelope with my name as the addressee badly misspelled in a crimpy hand. I know that the contents assured me of the untimely death by drowning of Ms. Juliette Tartan. That it happened at the fair. It will seem as though I am justifying my harmless fantasy by dint of absence of factual details. On the contrary; my shame lies in the current explanation and apology, attached with a garish and conspicuous bit of twine. But how else to make you flip back to the start, where I am grasping still through that surging crowd for that perennially absent wrist? To plead with me to extinguish an untimely cigarette from behind the muting curtain of years?

THE UNUSUAL NARRATIVE
OF THE ODESSA CONFERENCE

Dawnóż to było, gdy stałem pomiędzy nicością a krzyżem
Aleksander Wat

It is five years ago now that my university, the University of Central Canada, which enjoys the status of centrality neither in the literal nor the figurative sense, sent me at its own considerable expense to the 31st annual conference for the Promotion of Educated Discourse in faraway Odessa. I confess with a modicum of shame that I needed to consult my atlas with my wife . . . and that we started looking for Odessa in the wrong hemisphere. I found, to my considerable consternation, that not only was it a place that I had never heard of, but it was deep in the middle of a vast area about which I was equally ignorant. Somehow, the total absence of a friendly Halifax, Zurich, or even Calcutta amidst the dense clusters of Dnipopetrovs'ks, Tighinas, Arcyzes, and Mohyliv-Podil'kyjs gave me a profounder feeling of unrest than I had theretofore experienced prior to a journey, as though wandering alone into a thick, black forest with only a flickering candle of orientation in my pocket. My wife, Gloria, said that I was being silly. "Even in Odessa," she cooed, smoothing back my hair, "they will find you a flashlight."

That night, as I awoke squinting in the glare from a streetlamp beaming through the overhastily-drawn curtains, I began to trace my fingers down the uneven spine of my slumbering wife, and I thought clearly that mine were Canadian hands, and that the soft blue light whispering into the bedroom was a glow from a Canadian street and I memorized these things for recollection when I would be I didn't know where.

Leaving for the airport, my wife dressed me in my overcoat and hat. I seemed to have forgotten how to go about it with my own two hands. We drove the entire distance in a strange mute stupor stopping only for the traffic signals. When I hugged my wife good-bye I began sobbing softly. "Oh, now," she said curiously, "there have been other departures."

Between that and the boarding, in that strange intercontinental corridor, I smoked cigarettes savagely, one after another, a single refrain from some elusive book of poetry swimming in my head, "And that my ego, bound by no outward force . . . Should now seem strange to me, like a strange dog."

I was assigned to row thirty-four. Under my arm was a complimentary newspaper that I couldn't recall having taken. My seat was by the window, and to get to it meant the off-putting task of wedging myself past my neighbor-to-be's enormous, spread thighs. A minute later we had gruntingly negotiated our separate terrains, a process that had left him flushed and lightly dappled with sweat.

"I'm afraid I'm a size or two overgrown for these seats!" he jested in a rough British accent, at which I offered a weak smile and chuckled. "Usher's the name," he said, drawing a dog-eared business card from his breast pocket and slapping it down fondly onto my little plastic tray. I forcibly re-oriented myself out of my old frame of mind and into this new social predicament, and my eyes succeeded in focusing on the little card: "Clark Usher, General Sales Division, Ektop Ltd." "Ektop?" I mumbled, more to myself than to him, and then immediately wished I hadn't, as he saw this as an opening to illuminate the billions of drab and inconsequential details which, when clotted together like a child building a mud pie, had ossified into the indiscriminate unity of a life. Mr. Usher wore green suspenders and a necktie that was probably once capable of circumnavigating the great orb of his girth, but no more. He wore his sleeves rolled up and when he smiled — which was frequently — he exposed an uncommonly generous quantity of upper gums.

But happily, Mr. Usher was an alcoholic. I gave him my little cocktails to help him along, and after only two hours of unbroken autobiography he had fallen asleep in the upright position. It had by then gotten dark both inside and outside the fuselage, and the only sounds were the gentle, fluttery moans of passengers settling into an unfamiliar and murky species of sleep. I pressed a button on my armrest and was bathed in an island of light, one of an only four-strong archipelago onboard the plane. I softly unfolded the newspaper and with weary eyes skimmed for the gists of various international dramas. My gaze fixed on a bizarre item on page five.

"Tourists to Rats," read the headline. And below: "After the disappearance of seven more international tourists from Volgograd, positively identified as two Swedes, an American, and four Germans, an extraordinary letter appeared on our copy editor's desk. It stated that the travelers had been seized and held by force, drugged, and then turned, one by one, into rats. The author of the letter offered as proof an accompanying photograph of seven gray rats, most probably of the *glaucus mus* genus. Police are still pondering whether or not to take the letter seriously . . ."

"Oh, they'll have to take it seriously," wheezed Clark Usher, giving me a terrible jolt with his sudden, boozy presence, his two huge scarlet eyes glowing from outside the island of light. "I've seen this before . . . but it's always treated half in jest." His voice had developed an unsettling huskiness, and his face possessed a chiaroscuro macabre. "But mark my words . . . Eventually, when the number of wayward tourists climbs above fifty . . . and it surely will . . . then you'll see the bobbies poking around in the Volgograd gutters, trying to sift the real vermin from the travelers." He burst into a steady, prolonged laughter, like air escaping from the pinched end of a balloon. When he ran out he coughed and spluttered for a moment and then lit a cigarette, winking and offering me one. I gratefully accepted, and as I lit it my eyes fell upon the photograph of the rats, which stared towards the camera with wild and pleading expressions. Looking at their eyes I almost started to believe that they were German eyes, staring out from the middle-point of some unimaginable chaos, but then I righted my train of thought with a long suck on my cigarette. A low rumbling sound made me glance at Usher, who had fallen asleep with his lit cigarette dangling from his puffy lips. Flakes of ash fell like autumn leaves onto the downy meadow of his expansive belly. I gently removed the glowing remainder from his mouth, stubbed it out, and switched off the light overhead.

I was carrying something terribly heavy, something which dug into my shoulder blades, and suddenly I was aware that I was falling onto my knees except that there was nothing solid for my knees to fall onto and then I woke up to find the plane descending and Clark, his mouth full of croissant and scrambled egg, shaking me to secure myself for the imminent landing. Out the window the sun was scaling a powdery violet sky, and the perambulations of the morning traffic were just becoming visible. Clark Usher's face had undergone a remarkable transformation, had shed all of its nighttime monstrosity and regained its friendly though pallid composition. Stewardesses; runway; disembarking.

I remember neither my farewell to Clark nor the passport check area. My next memory is a surging mass of expectant families and friends. My eyes scanned the crowd for any academic-looking personae and rested on a young, dark-haired woman with square-rimmed glasses, holding aloft a sign with the crest of the International Society for the Promotion of Educated Discourse: two humanoid lions wrestling with each other, one's teeth locked in the other's shoulder, with a stylized globe hovering between them. She picked me out at once (perhaps because of my elevated forehead) and moved to assist me with my suitcases. Her name was Tatiana, and with her was a Norwegian professor of mystic philosophy who went by the name of Olaf. Olaf was obviously suffering from his flight, but he was not at all wanting in Scandinavian affability.

All of Odessa smelt of salt. The day was bright. "Odessa is a city conceived for dusk . . ." said Tatiana chimerically, but the oddest thing was that I intuited her meaning. The sunlight washed uneasily across the stone façades of buildings that twisted chaotically, like tangled roots bursting out of the uneven streets that led us downhill to the historic center of town.

Entering the fortified center necessitated going through an arch, carved onto which were the remnants of an inscription. Our guide translated as follows: "Odessa is the sound of the Gothic strings retuning." "You see . . ." explained Tatiana as Olaf dug flecks of dust from his left retina, "there was a belief that as Odessa was being built, the Gothic style had reached its pinnacle of expression. The air was thick with the conviction that the style had been exhausted, in literature, music, architecture . . ." We passed a fountain carved in the shape of a man posed in classic Grecian mid-sway, who held his own severed head under his arm. The open, grimacing mouth of the head vomited water into a basin below. Children kicked a ball around it. ". . . that anything that could come next would either need to be a sheer break from the Gothic, or else suffer the fate of being a meaningless repetition. History has generally been more kind. Some scholars describe our city as the last great flowering of the late Gothic period. Others, less charitably, as the Gothic style's last shriveled stump."

We wandered through a fresh fish market thick with crimson, long-bodied, winged insects, which seemed to flit about unnoticed by the shoppers and fishmongers alike. The latter all had overabundances of metal teeth, which made awful glares in the blanched sunlight. Dogs played with fish heads in the gutter. For a short time the all-pervading salt smell surrendered to that of moldering fish. Olaf and Tatiana maintained their brisk pace, but I lagged behind to closer inspect a gaping and slightly puckering carp maw. As I approached it, I watched my index finger slowly inch forwards and stick itself between the carp's undulating lips. The fish clamped down on it with surprising strength. Only then did I notice a fishmonger with a bloody smock and extensive dental reconstruction looming over me. I tried to look as dignified as possible with my finger inside the fish. "America?" said the man, leering crookedly. "As a matter of fact, no, I'm . . . no, Canada. CaNAda," I rattled, stifling the urge to tell him about the streetlamps and how with hands like these I ought to have been sent to piano lessons. "Canada. Ha ha ha ha," he chuckled monotonously, and then, his features having clouded somewhat, "Hey . . . you want buy . . . krysa? No . . . shchoor?" Then three things happened at exactly the same instant. A carpet of black clouds swept across the sky and tore open with rain. The fishmonger pounded the tail of the carp with his fist causing the mouth to snap open and my finger to be released. And Tatiana grabbed me by the elbow and pulled me away.

The Hotel Turichistesky was only one hundred meters away, but upon reaching its uniquely drab lobby, decorated exclusively in clashing shades of brown, the deeply rooted reek of old tobacco stains universal, a few shiftless characters slumped suspiciously in the only upholstered chairs, I was drenched and shivering. Olaf had already checked in and was unruffled by the lobby, scrutinizing an embroidered picture of galloping horses in a broken frame. I stood idly by, picking at the chipped varnish of the service desk as Tatiana and the hotel owner exchanged whirlpools of Slavic syllables.

Olaf and I were to share a room. Two beds separated by a plain wooden table on which sat a lamp that didn't work, a plywood wardrobe with one door halfway pulled off its hinges and three wire coat hangers that were fastened to the rack to deter would-be thieves, and, when the curtains were parted to yield a view of what might have been a grain elevator, they also revealed a massive radio that took up the entirety of the windowsill and had six more dials than I recalled a radio needing. Olaf flung himself down on the bed and gave out a cry of pain and surprise. Something metal had jabbed into his lower back.

The torrential rain refused to abate, so we were condemned to remain in our room. I tried in vain to concentrate on a book of applied narratology, Olaf made staticky sounds with the radio. Olaf smoked a cigarette ruminatively, I stared gloomily out the window. I tried out the radio, Olaf spread out and folded his collection of decorative socks. I hit upon some frequency which, from behind the warbling tenor of a Russian opera, one could just make out the pale traces of a news report in French.

"Comme j'ai déjà dit . . . le monde, sera le monde, après tout . . . en même temps, en Russie . . . il y a trente-et-un gens qui sont . . . avec une photo des rats . . . jamais . . ." I turned to Olaf for some reaction, but he was blithely folding socks on his knee and whistling along to the Shostakovich in the foreground. "What is your specialty in mystic philosophy," I asked. "I am a Plotonian," he said cheerily, and then, with a note of regret, "There are not many of us left."

At nine o'clock the rain had somewhat let up and our hunger had suddenly and decisively overcome us. The hotel restaurant was filled with guttersnipes and drunks, so we headed out into the drizzly night on our own.

The challenge proved to be in finding a place that was in fact a restaurant in the familiar sense of the word. We would bound over great, oily puddles, nearly topple down crumbling steps, and throw open some heavy medieval door only to be confronted with the same four or five, sullen, badly-shaven thugs murkily drinking pint-glasses of thick, transparent vodka. The moment that

Olaf would stroll in from the icy rain with his tourist shorts, long crimson legs and little tufts of creamy blonde hair at his kneecaps, the game was up.

Tatiana was correct. In the slippery lamplight Odessa's architectural peculiarities came to life. Its gargoyles squirmed fiendishly. The buildings seemed fluid and were always shifting about on you when they occupied the periphery of your vision. A file of orthodox Jews swept by muttering almost inaudibly, like a murder of crows. Or were they only the shadows of lampposts.

We swiftly lost our way, and then we were damp, morose, and totally uncommunicative in any language spoken for a thousand miles. But we finally happened upon a restaurant. The light came from a giant hearth in which cooked the half-carved shape of an animal roasted reddish-bronze. An inordinate number of policemen sat around the wobbly timber tables, many of whom chuckled under their breaths and nudged each other meaningfully when we sat ourselves down. Smoke hung thickly.

Olaf and I ordered some mid-priced entrees of entirely mysterious character and settled down at a corner table. At the far end of the restaurant I saw curtains that seemed to hint at a small stage. "Oho," I said to Olaf, "I think we're in for a performance."

No sooner had these words fluttered out of my lips like dusty moths than the curtains drew apart and the sound of dueling accordions filled the restaurant. On stage appeared a gentleman in tattered top hat and tails with a ghoulish smile painted bright red onto his cheeks. He introduced a series of attractions. First there was a contortionist with closely cropped black hair and nervously flickering eyes, who was capable of twisting his legs into such revolting postures that I was compelled to look away. Next up was an old bearded gentleman who made doleful noises by bowing and wiggling an iron saw. Olaf and I gave him our polite attention, but my mind had started freely associating, from the saw to my trembling knees in the dream on the airplane, to Clark Usher, to kissing my wife good-bye, to Gloria's baffled smile, to a night I had spent with her drinking red wine and laughing and crying to the very large portion of hot oily tripes that the waitress was setting before me. I had ordered it through cruel happenstance. The very smell was enough to make my sensitive throat go into convulsions. Olaf shifted a bit down the table with his roast pork to get away from the smell of my dish. At this point the music changed in texture and the lighting as well seemed to change. The tuxedoed man again appeared stage center and displayed that disagreeable grin of his. He went into a long comic speech that was well appreciated by the crowd, but was entirely lost on me. Olaf laughed mildly from time to time so as not to appear too ungrateful an audience, indulging his Scandinavian sense of propriety.

He looked absurd, larding the general merriment with his polite mirth. Most unsettling, though, was the fact that it seemed as if the comedian were inciting the crowd to laugh ominously while gesturing towards Olaf and myself. My senses may have been confused. I had choked back the last of my food, and a dull, warm, stupid feeling was spreading through my body, a torporous undertow brought on by the filling, hot tripes. A volunteer was being invited up to the stage, a young, dark waiter with blotchy skin. The presenter elicited a few more chuckles from the audience while the waiter agitatedly shifted from foot to foot, and then he drew out a long blade and lopped the boy's head from its shoulders. I squinted my throbbing eyes to see through the smoky haze. The youth had tucked his still-blinking head under one arm and was feeling his way offstage with the other amidst some stormy applause. "Olaf . . ." I heard my voice peep as the entertainer wheeled onstage a silver cage containing seven familiar-looking rats on top of a cart. And thereafter the rhythmic pounding of more applause was heard.

I jerked awake and found the plane descending and old Clark, his mouth brimming with croissant and scrambled egg, shaking me to secure myself for the imminent landing. I lunged at him and seized him by the stiffened collar, causing his coffee to slosh treacherously to and fro on his dining tray. "Tell me what you know about the rats" I murderously growled, causing other passengers to look in our direction. Mr. Usher just stared at me, unpeeling my fingers from his collar and suggesting that perhaps the arduousness of traveling had put me off-color. The night's sleep had left him more British.

We disembarked separately without so much as a polite word of farewell. My stomach felt as though it were trying to digest a live animal. The customs officer had difficulty matching my badly-shaven and nausea-distorted face with the serene and smiling one in the passport. My suitcases were slashed open with a practiced swipe of a razor blade, rifled through, and then resealed with electrical tape.

A raven-haired woman named Tatianna was waiting for me in the arrival hall, holding up a sign emblazoned with the crest of the International Society for the Promotion of Educated Discourse: two humanoid lions devouring each other's tails, with a stylized globe hanging between them. With her was a professor of applied metaphysics from the Central University of Norway, who affably introduced himself as Olaf.

Everywhere you walked in Odessa you stepped in mud up to your ankles. Thus, a revolting squelching noise was ubiquitous. My suitcase on wheels, purchased at great cost, sank so deeply at one point that I was forced to abandon it. The buildings, some of which built in the shape of great, yawning gargoyle heads, leaned disarmingly this way or that, and things like potted plants or children's toys were forever sliding off of balconies and onto the streets below, gravely injuring passers-by.

"Tatianna . . ." I began, but then stopped myself, hearing my thin voice echo like a rubber ball through alleyways, over rooftops, into the courtyards and sewers. We arrived at a great hexagonal piazza surrounded by structures that seemed too old to be standing. The wind couriered a creaking sound. Wooden planks were laid over the piazza, stretching from one end to the other. The mud here had reached such depths that it could not be safely trod upon.

The planks teetered unsteadily under our cautious footsteps. Olaf chuckled good-naturedly to dispel the general gloom. We had to interrupt our progress from time to time as people crossed planks laid crosswise to ours, grave and vampiric shadows of people often dressed in cloaks. At one such intersection we passed a group of filth-covered farmers, their arms filled with squealing and clawing livestock. As they passed us, a corpulent piglet kicked its way free and leapt onto our plank, causing it to shake terribly and setting us all off balance. At just that precarious moment an undernourished hen seized the opportunity to wrench itself from its owner's arms, flapping squarely into my aghast face. It was in this way that I fell into the waiting mud with a brief wail that got stuck in my throat. Up to my chest and slowly sinking in the historic center of Odessa, I wiped the grime from my eyes and saw Olaf's long and veiny Scandinavian arm stretched out towards me to offer help, only inches too short. The hen had fallen headfirst into the mud and, to judge by the motionlessness of her legs, had already suffocated. Tatianna searched in vain for a stick, and as I felt the mud resolutely ooze up over my shoulders I thought to myself that this, too, must have a bottom.

I came to with a thunderous pulse raging in the brain-pan and a soft blue light coming in through the window, and for a fleeting moment I thought: Oh, thank God, I'm in Canada. But then I saw Olaf's sturdy frame slumped in the corner opposite, little rivulets of blood at his temples and felt the ground shuddering beneath me and I pieced together that I was in the back of a transport vehicle being taken somewhere. I had the sickly aftertaste of tripes at the back of my throat and my clothing was encrusted in dried mud, all of it. I peered out the bar-covered window and there was the heavy form of the moon, the source of the watery-blue light I had mistaken for Canada. Olaf was dreaming badly, and his periodic whimpers sent chills of recognition down my spine. "Olaf . . ." I stage-whispered, ". . . Olaf, what's happened to us . . . there was a mud-pit . . . and a restaurant . . ."

"Oh, God, the restaurant!" he wailed, his eyelids

fluttering in a state of collision or confrontation between dream and waking, unable to select which was the more perfidious. "The man with one glass eye is lifting the shroud from the box . . . he intends to commit unclean acts . . . the man with one glass eye has tricked God into paralysis . . . he is clothed like a lion . . . when he smiles there is malice . . . Oh! Vermin! . . ." Here the truck hit a bump and Olaf's fragile condition was irrevocably disrupted.

Inside of five minutes I had oriented Olaf to the situation at hand and his stare had lost most of its glassy despondency. We had very little difficulty in untying each other (Olaf had trained seven years with the Norwegian boy scouts), and this small victory put us in fine spirits. Olaf found a little flask of powerful liquor in his shirt pocket and we gulped it back like giddy adolescents. Whereupon Olaf lifted up one of his giant, steel-toe booted legs and vigorously kicked open the back doors.

It was like the curtains opening to show the fantastical set of a play! Snow shimmered all about, painted in blues by the moonlight, geese flew overhead, the road slid from under the truck at an electric speed. The landscape was so austere, I swear I was more afraid of finding myself in the heart of it than I was of being in that really rather cozy truck . . . But as it turned out, the choice was not mine to make. In a moment Olaf had seized me bodily and thrown me headlong into a snowdrift. Flushed with excitement, I picked myself up from the ground and turned back to see a struggling Olaf being dragged back into the truck, still speeding away, and the back doors slamming shut. My exhilarated grin faded into the icy fields of my new reality.

I struck out into the motionless landscape, feeling the vague and pulsating warmth of Olaf's alcohol in my veins, watching my long pianist's fingers turn blue from the cold. Every direction was equally desolate. I would take a dozen steps one way, be overcome by hopelessness, start out on another tack, the same thing . . . As I stumbled forth I drew a line map of my progress in my head, sketching out the trail by which I'd come in dark charcoal across the blank canvas of my thoughts, all the way from the truck to some future point which I marked with an optimistic "x" . . . and little by little, with my nose numbing to a tender rose and the wind muttering obscenities in my ears, little by little I began re-orienting my focus of attention away from the robotic plod of my fur-lined boots through the snow and the moon satelliting through the firmament far above, away from these things and deeper inward, into the very trails of the map I was drawing, a map which was becoming three-dimensional . . . The charcoal blackness, upon drawing closer to it, dissolved into filigrees which obscured camps of huddled people, bundled in wools and sitting by dark orange gas lamps, holding each other by the hand and kissing each other on the forehead.

I wake up amongst some trash cans in an alley that reeks of old booze and filth. Alternatively, the smell may be coming from me. I remember very little, but I have the absolute certainty that I am in Volgograd. I am in Volgograd and the rat people will be trying to find me.

My pants are torn and my collar is weirdly askew. The more I tug at it, the more I disfigure it. I scuttle crustaceously along unfamiliar streets pulling at the stubble on my face. A man gives me a cigarette, which I smoke energetically. I reel off the street and into a coffeehouse teeming with suspect clientele. From the menu bordered with turn-of-the-century lilies, I locate coffee, which is bitter and arrives in a glass with no handle and a thick layer of grounds clogging up the top. I pull my battered edition of *Applied Narratology* out of my pocket, thinking that I might try to anchor myself in something direct and rational, that I might read something that would make sense of my disarray. "Focalization," I read, "is the relationship between the 'vision', the agent that sees (the focalizor), and that which is seen." I skim on past the bits on analepsis and prolepsis, and read the following, "If the retroversion occurs within the time span of the primary fabula, then we refer to an internal analepsis . . . If the retroversion begins outside the primary time span and ends within it, we refer to a mixed retroversion." I hear a rustling noise and look up to see a man sitting across from me. He is dressed in a tan winter coat with an extravagant fur collar. There is a fedora on his head and a pair of costly sunglasses on his face. He is agitatedly chewing on a lump of sugar. "You are in unspeakable danger here," he hisses from between clenched teeth, and it makes me jump in my seat to hear English being spoken. "The problem is in the fact," he says leaning forward, beckoning me closer, his voice a conspiratorial whisper, "that you are incapable of dreaming the Crimea. But I will help you to get a foothold. Don't drink that coffee, it will only make things worse . . ."

The stranger leads me along boulevards filled with rumbling automobiles and trains, outside of the city center and into the lobby of a post-secession tenement building. We go upstairs without a word exchanged between us, and at the very top there is his apartment. I scarcely register the squalid poverty of the decor, the broken furniture and the smell of rot. The stranger shows me to a low, concave bed and I immediately black out from sheer exhaustion.

"Ektop?" I hear myself saying, and that one word, like a refrain from a melody one has known since childhood, tells me everything I will find around me when I lift my weary head. "Ektop isn't just another business," recited Usher, his brow furrowing earnestly, "It's a philosophy."

Clark snored a basso continuoso to my left as I pushed a button on my armrest, thereby illuminating my seating-area. I could scarcely believe that I was back on that infamous airplane, opening up the very same newspaper, hurtling towards the next, consecutive Odessa. I flipped past the now-familiar "Tourists to Rats" piece, and my gaze rested on a small item near the back. It was the 100th anniversary of the death of Poland's national poet. He had lived through a turbulent era and was responsible for the idea that every nation, every generation, and beyond that, every single individual walks his or her own stations of the cross. I stopped reading as this idea rippled and resonated in my mind. I was normally suspicious of poetry, but somehow, on that night . . . I closed the newspaper softly, so as not to rouse the dreaming Mr. Usher, and clicked off the overhead light. The stars were all where they ought to have been, and the airplane engine hummed a lullaby.

My first thought was: I am falling once more. And then there was Clark, with his half-chewed eggs and croissant. And the descent.

Tatiana was there waiting for me in the arrivals lounge, albeit oddly Olafless, and holding aloft the crest of the International Society for the Promotion of Educated Discourse: a humanoid lion greedily devouring its own tail. As we made our way through the airport, my absurd little suitcase rolling in our wake, I slowly came to recognize that everyone about us was wearing plastic masks, molded to take on human features. I mentioned this observation to Tatiana, to which she replied, "Yes . . . they are all giant rats." She contributed nothing more on the subject, and I feared it was too culturally sensitive to delve further.

It was the same thing in the streets, everyone bent-backed and wearing grinning plastic masks and long, yellow overcoats. I tried to catch sight of a tail dragging behind one of them to back up Tatiana's peculiar claim, but this ended in vain. Perhaps they wind them up inside their coats, I resolved. We passed through a great stone archway that led us to the historic town center, an archway inscribed with a motto that Tatiana translated as signifying "Odessa is the sound of the Gothic wires snapping." "You'll have plenty of opportunities to see that arch again," said my guide with a chimeric grin. Soon I understood her immaculately. We went through that archway three, four, six times, always from the same side, and then I lost count of how many passes we had made. "Tatiana . . ." I croaked, keeping my voice low so as not to tip off the rats, who would surely take me for an American, ". . . we are moving in circles." The sound of my own voice seemed strange to me. Tatiana giggled.

"Foreigners always think that at first. Pay more attention."

Absolutely right, I thought to myself, keen attention

to detail is what this situation requires. During our next pass I noted that just beyond the archway was a boy selling newspapers, a small pile of kopeks in front of him on a small dish. His knee-length pants were torn horribly and he had very large ears and a mustard-yellow cap. I committed these things to memory. Now we'll see if there is one archway or many, I vowed, wondering what Heraclitus or Nietzsche would have made of my empirical philosophizing. When we passed the gate once more I eagerly looked for my newsboy. He was right where we had left him, but . . . his cap was pumpkin-orange. I tried to recall what Berkeley had said, that colors, as secondary substances, existed only in the mind . . . but the significance of the cap's transformation . . . what it meant for the archway, for Odessa, and ultimately, myself even . . . seemed entirely beyond reckoning.

But then suddenly we were at the hotel "Tourist," and I was swept by a wave of morbid anxiety at the thought of being left alone, of the prospect of falling asleep and waking up in God knows which Odessa, totally alone and stranded with my electrical-tape repaired and fishy-smelling suitcase-on-wheels and my hands that were so disfigured that I wished I were wearing gloves. Tatiana laughed with a kindly lilt, straightened out my collar, and gave me a little flashlight (embossed with the lion insignia) to give me courage throughout the night, which, she added unnecessarily, was to be the longest of the year.

I lay feverishly, incurably awake until three a.m., in dread expectancy of forthcoming Odessas, not entirely able to decide if I was trapped in not being able to leave Odessa, or rather that my trap was in my inability to definitively arrive, calling up fragments of literature like holy spirits to soothe me and stave off the shadows: "One is a superfluous mist, a little puff of breath exhaled, which God no longer bothers about"; "This continuous whittling away of his personality seemed linked to a vague presage of the rebuilding elsewhere of a personality"; "I could write a treatise / on the sudden change / of life to archaeology"; "Do thyself no harm! For we are all here!" And then it was three o'clock.

I woke up amidst snowdrifts. The numbness of my extremities indicated that I had been unconscious for some time. Every bone yearned to escape the cold, and I reflected that I might have spent the previous night in the hotel Tourist a good bit more merrily had I known what the bitter sequel would bring.

The sound of a motor was just audible in the distance. There might be somebody who would drive me to a warm place, I thought. Yet I was entirely consumed in blackness. I found myself quickly recalling everything: Olaf in the truck, falling out, losing Olaf, trudging hopelessly from nowhere to nowhere. I shouted at the vehicle as much as my throat would allow, but my voice was carried away by the wind. My left hand half-somnambulantly reached into a pocket and fished out Tatiana's flashlight. It seemed to me that there might be a dubious narrative congruity to the flashlight being in my pocket at that moment . . . but then I was delirious from the cold and the disorientation . . . in any case, I raised the thing above me like the torch of liberty and waved it about energetically. I heard the screech of brakes as the car pulled to a halt. The strength in my limbs, attenuated to a virtual abyss by the cold, rallied for a sprightly hobble to the road.

The motorist was a gentleman of Scythian profile and manner. His automobile, mercifully, was equipped with a small vent that coughed up petroleum-smelling hot air, and I placed my hands greedily over this as I hopped into the car. As soon as I shut the door, we were off. It occurred to me that I remembered from somewhere the Russian word for "where." Pointing through the windshield and into the swirling murk and haze so as to indicate our destination, I slurred "Giddy-eh?" through my frozen lips. There was an unnaturally protracted pause, during which time I expectantly studied the driver's features, his sad and drooping eyebrows, the gradual and chiseled ascension of his forehead, the lumpy contours of his skull, the skyward swoop of his nose, and without determining what on earth for, I found myself bringing my index finger closer to his expansive mouth, to wedge it between his full Slavonic lips, until he burst out with "Volgograd!" so abruptly and ghoulishly that it made me spring back, and again, "Volgograd!" and then neither of us knew what to say or do for the next three hours of driving.

Getting out of that singular automobile I felt distinctly like a strange replica or parody of myself. The stubble on one side of my face had grown more quickly than on the other, my breath stank of booze and exhaustion and I favored my right leg as I walked, a result of having fallen badly out of the truck. I avoided staring at people directly, though the few denizens awake at that bitterly early hour were just as unsightly as I. For half an hour I limped through the city of Volgograd, where the leaves of trees were painted gray to avoid striking a discordant note with the buildings, and at long last I found a solitary alleyway where I happily nestled myself between a pair of trash cans, in the cloying odor of refuse, for a tempestuous sleep.

Waking up this time felt like a struggle of will, an unwieldy tug, as though there existed a muscle that was used to dormancy but yet was necessary to launch my consciousness from the thick bog in which it was embedded. When I finally succeeded and my eyes sprung open I felt all through my body a narcotic heaviness. I recognized the room to be the one to which the stranger in the café had led me, and I was reassured in connecting a memory to the present. I heard deliberate footsteps enter the room, drawers sliding open and shut, all outside of my frozen periphery. A breakdown of focalization, I mused, due to the paralysis of the focalizor. But then he was right on top of me, the man from the café, who was removing his sunglasses to get a closer look at me and revealing to my dumbstruck terror one perfectly good eye and one glass eye, and all at once Olaf's twilight back-of-the-truck prophecy leapt to mind, and it occurred to me that the stranger's abundant fur collar was not unlike the mane of a lion, a second confirmation of the prophecy, and were it not for my total powerlessness, my complete corporal paralysis, I would certainly have lunged off of the low, concave bed, or wrapped my slender Canadian hands around his neck, or, at the very least, shuddered in horror. As it stood, I lay extremely still. A boiled cabbage smell was wafting into the room, my nose informed me, and a woman and a man were muttering to each other. The lion was still staring at me, and I found the thought crossing my mind that he was scrutinizing me so intently because I had been turned into a rat. Now, at first I chuckled (silently) at this auto-suggestion, what could be more absurd after all, but the seeds of anxiety had been planted, resolutely, incontrovertibly, in my mind, and I could not prove through my senses that I was either rat or man because I could not see my body and I could not feel the parts from, as it were, inside. I wracked my tired, swampy mind for some way to prove my humanity simply by use of my unaided reason, to establish through the interworkings of my consciousness that I was an elevated specimen on the Great Chain of Being; I tried to recall what various philosophers had said on the subject, on what separates man from the squalid dross of the animal kingdom . . . but I could summon to mind not a whit of comfort. The situation was clearly preposterous. Could a mere rat unnerve itself in such a base and infamous fashion? But on the other hand, what better example of bestial irrationality?! While my wits jousted thusly, scoring points and then losing them, along came the lion, his face wrought with a decorative smile, holding a thick black cloth. This he tenderly laid over my face. And then, as if through suggestion or enchantment, I felt a great need for sleep, all at once, and somewhere I even felt relief at the notion that my personality would emerge from this, too, into a place that I was incapable of imagining, that I would ebb into slumber only under this firm condition, that I would come forth, re-emerge, into a place that had certainties.

A CUP OF COFFEE
IN THE EVENING

Roger moved into a new apartment at the corner of 73rd Avenue and Vine Street, a standard one-room with white-washed walls and standard, if plain, furnishings. Shortly after moving in he felt slightly ill, and it was with some pleasure that he called in sick to the burnt sugar factory where he daily earned his paychecks, looking forward to a minor reprieve from his routine. He was surprised by the stillness he felt in his new home, the unshakable feeling of absence that permeated the very air. It scared him, yet it was invigorating to be frightened.

Roger was unaccustomed to drinking coffee in the evenings, knowing full well the toll that it took on his nerves. And yet this particular evening he was unable to resist. He took up a string of minutes watching it percolate and took little sips so as not to burn the lips and roof of the mouth.

Through the window the sun was threatening to set. It loitered murkily over the horizon, a shadow of its former self, bleached by the haze manufactured by the ever-present city lurking in wait beneath. Roger absent-mindedly stirred his coffee with a finger, sniffling wretchedly and trying to catch a glimpse of his own factory far in the distance. It was no use. The haze was simply too thick.

Positioned opposite the kitchen window was a long and narrow mirror. Roger lifted the rim of his upper lip to expose the gums, which he thought to be suffering from discoloration. "The key to health lies in the gums," Mum had often recited, mentioning as verification that her cousin's gums had been simply yellow the day he passed away from some silent disease. Standing in front of the mirror, the entirety of his upper lip flipped up grotesquely, Roger noticed something curious. The sun was considerably brighter in the mirror than it was through the window. In the mirror it shimmered and sparkled merrily . . . why, it even winked at him. Roger took another good, hard look out the window to confirm this impression. The sun itself was as drab and mono-chromatic as ever.

Roger shifted around some boxes until he found the one in which he had packed his set of encyclopedias. "If you own a set of encyclopedias," the salesman had boasted, "you don't need any other books. They're all contained in here! But with . . . concision!" And it was the truth! Roger had never heard the word "concision" prior to that moment, but he remembered it even now. He opened the box with a straight edge razor and found the volume marked L-M in gold-embossed lettering. It pleased Roger to finger the pages of such a heavy, such a meaningful and above all well-bound volume. MIRROR.

"Invented quite by accident by Sir Alfred Cartwright, mason, who one evening noticed a charming effect when . . . etc., etc., . . . types of mirrors include . . . mirrors in literature generally foreshadow . . . etc., etc., . . . peculiar properties of the common household mirror abound . . ."

"Ah, here we are," thought Roger, rubbing his yellowish hands together.

". . . Reginald Wilkit first noticed what he was to thereafter label the 'Wilkit Effect,' whereby a beam of light striking a mirror at a very particular angle actually enters the texture of the mirror's surface and rebounds, plays off itself, and eventually creates a sharper or sometimes more vibrant image than the source itself. Wilkit confirmed this hypothesis by placing a second mirror across from one already impregnated by the Wilkit Effect, and the second mirror reproduced the image with an even more enhanced verisimilitude than the first. As Milton once so poetically stated . . ."

Roger slapped the book shut with a satisfied smile. He knew that there had had to be an explanation. The Wilkit Effect!

He slept very badly that night. Certainly the coffee hadn't helped things, but on top of that he felt as though something were tugging at him from the back of his mind, something imperative, which could spell trouble for him if he weren't cautious. But what on earth could it be?

As Roger awoke, he noted with displeasure that his condition had worsened. The simple act of raising his throbbing head from the pillow resulted in a kicking pain and a sense of uncontrollable vertigo. He wasn't able to summon the strength to leave the moist sanctuary of his bed until one o'clock in the afternoon. "Well," he muttered with a philosophical gravity, "age steals up on us all, eventually." Only then did he recall the Wilkit Effect, and hurried to the kitchen to see if perhaps there was further evidence of it in today's mirror.

And indeed, there was. The dismal townscape appeared as apocalyptic as ever through the fly-blown window, but under the mirror's lyrical afternoon sun the building-tops glimmered as though dappled with pixie-dust. It pleased Roger to see them there, iridescent and smiling, and he congratulated himself on his discovery of the Effect. At which point something odd caught his attention. He thought he noticed a small, cumulonimbus cloud in the mirror, though it was not actually in the sky proper, that is to say, seen through the window. At first he was certain that he had merely gotten confused, that because the mirror was reflecting everything backwards, or front to back, that he was simply looking for the cloud in the wrong patch of sky-through-the-window. Yet, after consulting with the window and the mirror four or five times, he was convinced that this was not the case. The cloud was only in the mirror, drifting confidently over the faultlessly polished skyline, just like a cloud would do in real life. He sat and watched it for some time, but in no way did it do anything surprising. He sat with his eyes fixed on it though, until it floated outside of the frame of the mirror. CLOUD.

"Composition of . . . significance when beheld . . . various types of . . . how to read . . . affiliated optical illusions:

"Clouds not perceptible to the human eye may from time to time appear in transfigurations of sky (see also: the principles of A. Schönberg). This phenomenon was first observed by Sir Edwin Grant, who took a photograph of an airplane traveling through a clear blue sky, and developed the negatives to find the whole of the image of the aircraft obliterated by clouds. The theory applied may strike us as overly straightforward, yet it holds. The rays of the sun shining through an ultra-fine cloud-surface renders the latter translucent to the normal series of optical processes, as an over-accumulation of sunbeam clogs up the lens of our vision, not leaving us the requisite 'space' with which to perceive the cloud. A camera, however, is not so easily tricked, and will record the errant cloud every time. The same process has been noticed on the surface of lakes, as well as in mirrors (see under: MIRROR; Peculiar properties: 'The Wilkit Effect')."

It was with some inner tribulation that Roger ever-so-carefully replaced the CA-EX volume of the encyclopedia. Despite the assurance of an overly-simplistic explanation, Roger had read the passage three times over and still felt unsure. How, in fact, did one's eyes get "clogged up?" Nonetheless, he was comforted that the sudden appearance of phantom clouds had found its way into the vast corpus of human knowledge, that a precedent had been set.

In the days that immediately followed, Roger became more and more preoccupied with the strange machinations of the Wilkit Effect. His whole days were spent in careful study of the increasingly brazen confabulations of the reality that was represented by his window in the slender room of his mirror. One afternoon a small framed picture appeared on one of the reflected walls of his kitchen. Close scrutiny, aided by a magnifying glass, revealed it to be a painting, a landscape bestrewn with trees, a hastily rendered sky with its electric blue and two misplaced clouds loitering one-dimensionally in the foreground. Finally, there was a doe in the moment of gentle prostration so inevitable in such paintings, its lithe neck curved in the act of lapping water from the nearby brook. A signature at the bottom of the painting was so faint that one could not be certain that one was reading it correctly: H. Gulya. The indubitability of the painting's reflection, i.e., its presence in the mirror, was sufficient alone to make Roger a shade uneasy. But what was more, there were no clouds or frolicsome deer reflected on the surface of the painted brook.

But this was not to be the most extraordinary event. The window in the mirror gradually became a surreal landscape, to which Roger became daily more and more transfixed. He witnessed violent crimes on the streets below, a man walking tightrope between two buildings, a flurry of bats knocking each other about and then vanishing to the unknown country outside of the frame. When a deep scarlet fog drifted in and covered his view for a few hours he continued watching, not wanting to be away for a moment if the view should all of a sudden clear up. His patience was rewarded when his view returned with a sky full of silken threads. He no longer bothered to ascertain if the image in the mirror corre-lated with the view from the window. One cannot be certain if the distinction was any longer relevant.

The threads sparkled and swayed in the mid-morning sun. Roger vaguely recognized a light breeze playing betwixt the hairs at the back of his neck. The sunny air caused a peculiar tingling sensation. He had maintained his vigil all through the night, and his head hurt like the devil, owing in part, no doubt, to the illness that was preying on his marrow. A brigade of armed soldiers was wending up avenues like the tail of some enormous rat. Tiny green caterpillars began spiraling down the threads hanging from the sky, some of which began cocooning in midair.

Roger gave his head a shake and had an unexpected moment of lucidity. The events accumulating, amassing before his blood-shot eyes, began to make him feel uneasy once more. He would have to slip on his coat and go to the library, that was all there was to it.

Roger made his way down identical boulevards, through the inevitable crowd of faces spilling out of doorways and from around corners, its collective voice a steady mechanized hum. He felt out-of-sorts, after a few blocks he already yearned for his chair in front of the mirror. He felt unsteady on his feet, and a dull throbbing below the left ear kept ruining his concentration. Happily, the library was nearby.

The Wilkit Effect: An Appraisal had been misshelved and he wasted fifteen minutes in tracking it down. At long last the librarian located it in the Astronomy section

. . . Someone had evidently mistaken it for a book about the Witkins Effect, which concerns visible shifts in sky conditions, wherein stars appear to move while in fact remaining stationary. Roger put the Wilkit book under his arm and stole off to a corner of the library. Chapter 14: SUPER-ABUNDANCE OF THE WILKIT EFFECT:

"In an extreme minority of recorded cases (which are themselves in the minority of daily recorded events), the Wilkit Effect has assumed greater proportions, thereby blooming into something unforeseen. Mr. Howard Pilkins of Zig-zag, Alabama, and Miss Ilona Konrad of Pecs, Hungary, have likewise reported what began as standard Wilkit Effects but then turned into more dramatic displays of mirrored illusion. We may doubt that Mr. Pilkins actually saw his deceased grand-mother dressed in a rose-colored wedding gown, but Miss Konrad's detailed description of the Gulya painting that suddenly came to adorn her bathroom wall surprises us, as she was otherwise unfamiliar with 18th-century art. Curiously, both Pilkins and Konrad have reported the onset of strange and disorienting attacks of illness after their respective experiences of the Super-abundant Wilkit Effect (S-aWE). If we were to express what we have discussed mathematically, we would arrive at the follow-ing theorem: . . ."

Thereafter, Roger's eyes blurred horribly as he scanned alien symbols whose significance he was not capable of divining. All of the carefully arranged x's and y's and %'s smoothed together into a pulpy mush of confusion. Exasperatingly, he could not recall if his illness had begun before or after he had first observed the Wilkit Effect. Before leaving the library he consulted one final book.

Hrath Gulya: The Man, the Paintings was the only relevant title available, and a slim volume at that. His fingers blundered through the glossy color reproductions until they rested at the very one he had seen in his mirror such a short time ago. A thorough examination showed it to be identical, in every detail, save that the deer was facing the other way, and the forested part of the landscape was to be found on the left-hand side, not the right. On the opposing page, Roger read the following:

". . . and yet, however, what strikes us in Gulya foremost is that which is conspicuously lacking. The artist consciously omits innovation, invention . . . creation, even, one might say, replicating a stock assortment of pedestrian images that in lesser (i.e., more one-dimensional) hands would result in mere sentimental humbuggery. And it is precisely in this self-censorship that the genius of Gulya's craft lies. One is forever aware of the percolating mastery that is persistently withheld from the surface of the canvas, forever denied the art admirer's searching gaze. And thereby the viewer is liberated from the conventional hierarchy of artist and audience . . . one is in fact blissfully at liberty to create the substance of the implied, unexecuted painting for oneself, unrestrained. Gulya's real paintings, then, achieve perfection in the whirling infinity of their non-existence."

Roger's eyes shot back and forth in his skull. He absent-mindedly replaced the book in a hole in the Selenography section and left the wanton confusion of the library, vowing not to return.

On the reeking flight of stairs leading to the door of his apartment, Roger stopped to feel the temperature of his forehead with the back of his hand. He found it to be radiating a sickly warmth. Moreover, there was an odd rattling inside his cranium like a gourd containing a few dried beans, and the vein below his right ear felt as though it were threatening to burst.

The key turned, the door swung open on faultless hinges, and Roger was at once assailed by a smell like that of a great accumulation of moldering books. His room was filled with a thousand monarch butterflies, a hopeless, breathless, utterly silent fluttering that did not even disturb the leaden air of the apartment. A hundred or so had found the encyclopedias and were diligently chewing holes in them with the aid of their little mandibles. Roger felt a trembling in his heart as the tiny creatures all lifted ceilingward in unison. The pounding of his pulse resonated through the whole of his disease-enfeebled body, with the shadow of his fever hanging over it all. He grasped at the left, then the right side of his chest, trying to feel the thump of his distressed heart behind the collision of bones, and then his legs gave way and he fell helplessly to the shallow carpet, either dead or in an exhausted faint.

A HYMN TO MILLIONAIRES

A few months ago, a working-class man with an amusing
lisp turned up at the entrance to the properties, offering
to triple-reinforce the doors against all manner of
intruder for a scoffingly low sum of money, so little in
fact that I was given cause to wonder if Count Mayberly,
self-proclaimed "irrepressible wit," had put the poor lad
up to it. But on second thought, he was simply too
authentic . . . far too many teeth crammed into his little,
puckered oral cavity, manure-encrusted, knee-high
Wellingtons, and eyes that knew only one direction
(dead ahead) and one expression (vacuity). All of which
meant that I did not engage his services, though my
doors are not as secure as they might be, because who
can say what kind of trouble that creature might get up

to on my properties, to say nothing of the low gossip if anyone saw him in my employ. I didn't even shake his hand, leaving that chore to the propitiously-gloved butler.

Of course, now that the hounds are ravenously throwing their sinewy bodies against the flimsily-bolted door of my study, my study which has not been blessed with a single window or a secondary exit, their strangled and bloodthirsty yowls resounding throughout the properties, I am wondering at the propriety of my decision. I estimate that the door is solid enough to keep the hounds at bay for somewhat less than an hour. After that, I am in God's big hands.

I note with some irritation that my genuine Persian-silk dressing gown, a gift from the Lebanese ambassador during his week-long visit for which I arranged hunts involving the very same breed of dog, by virtue of its superior strength of jaw and sharpness of tooth, that is currently pawing wildly at my door, has been dappled with blood below the left ribs. The little crimson flecks, already drying to a thick and powdery layer, open a floodgate of *memoria* not long past yet strangely remote-seeming. There I am, your narrator, arms flung wide to either side, an expression of unbridled terror clouding my perfectly-symmetrical features, a smattering of perspiration bejewelling my brow, my robe billowing majestically to the aft as I streak down a corridor resplendent with early-Rococo gilded latticework and priceless paintings.

I whistle past one of the hired help, who is bearing aloft a magnificent silver tray wrought with ornamentation and laden with cream-filled tarts, only the freshest cream, and persuade him to step in the way of the hounds nipping at my heels. This he does at once, first carefully setting aside the tray, then arranging his limbs for the imminent confrontation. He was the very model of stoicism, Leopold was, until the last. The dogs threw themselves upon him and he seemed to drown under their seething bodies, geysers of blood shooting in all directions, one of which caught me, as I have said, on the left breast of my robe.

When I first engaged Leopold he was scarcely thirteen, with a ruddy complexion and surprisingly adequate manners for a lad reared in the mildewy remotia of Poland. Yet there was doubtless no shortage of refinement to be done, and seeing as the boy was utterly cut adrift, I consented to allow him residence and training on my properties in exchange for unquestioning life-long devotion. He agreed at once. Leopold was one of my unconditional successes. He learned with swiftness and ease, and soon the only trace of his former life was a proclivity for beet-root soup and a mild Slavic accent, which the ladies of the properties found to have a rustic charm. Well do I recall a handful of nights when, having been granted permission to set aside his work for a moment, Leopold would entertain a company of noblemen and their wives, who had gathered around a crackling fireplace (with tumblers of brandy to warm the intestines) by telling tales of his dark and unthinkable homeland. He would tell of snowdrifts, of wolves and silhouettes of witches flying before the full moon, of strange customs and vulgar traditions. Invariably it would end with some fragile-tempered baroness, her pulse thundering from the terrible stimuli, swooning in the crashing tides of her own imagination. I would take the opportunity to call an end to the storytelling, dismissing Leopold and extinguishing the fire.

One evening, I distinctly recall it being Mrs. Saltern whose frail temperament put a stop to Leopold's tales. But of course, on this occasion it was sheer pretext. Her pug-nosed and thickly-mustachioed husband had savored one toddy too many, and was snoring resonantly on my bearskin carpet. All evening Mrs. Saltern had been imploring me with her eyes, regaling me with looks that demonstrated clear disgust with her husband's behavior, looks that unambiguously signified "So you see what I daily endure?" Thus, when she swooned at my butler's story and requested that I take her upstairs . . . let us say that I had forecast this eventuality.

Up, up the lovingly-carpeted and oak-banistered staircase I carried my houseguest's wife, noting her heaving bosom nested like robin's eggs within the infinitude of folds of her crinoline gown. My legs gathered speed as we floated down a long and tapestried corridor hung with chandeliers.

A word on those tapestries.

I cannot summon to mind a tapestry maker outside of the formidable Arguld whose name appears in a popular lyric of his day.

> . . . but full paynefull would mine hart be rent
> If Arguld hayn't come afore
> And spun his gilden threads a'lore
> Which quoth the baptiste, be angel-sent

It just so happens that the country's most extensive collection of Argulds can be found on my properties. The reason for this may arouse some interest.

My father was a lucky man, but profoundly dim when it came to matters of estate, administration, and, generally speaking, power. Many a time did I emerge from his den, my face smoldering red from some new difference of views, my patience having arrived at its very limits. On these occasions I would retire to my room and pound at a wall manfully, with both my fists, producing a sound not unlike that of the hounds still scrabbling away at the portal to my study. To resume: he was a lucky man, and one afternoon a merchant came along wanting to sell my father what he believed to be worthless tapestries, and at an extortionate price. I immediately recognized the items as priceless Argulds, while also noticing that the merchant was bluffing and did not know the worth of his wares. My role, then, was to convince the merchant that I genuinely thought the tapestries to be worthless yet interesting, while also not allowing him to guess my lie, lest he guess the true value of the tapestries, and moreover that I hadn't detected *his* bluff — a triple lie — because by threatening his integrity I would ruin any hope of a sale.

If this was confusing for myself, the rhetorical knot was nigh impossible for my father, bumbling oaf that he was. We took our leave of the merchant under some pretext and I tried to coach my father in the art of persuasion. He deigned not to listen. I was but nineteen at that time, yet I knew when it was time to take matters into my own hands. I implored the merchant to rest for supper, that we might better consider his offer.

Then I made to the kitchen, where the daily evening meal, suitable for the most discriminating of gourmands, was in the mid-stages of preparation. I espied the head chef, tall, lank, and olive-skinned, a refugee from some Mediterranean province, stirring a pot of bubbling sauce. I handed him a vial of aquamarine powder and commanded him to sprinkle it generously on the guest's platter.

Scene two takes place in the dining room, a small masterpiece of refined subtlety in the over-cluttered arena of decorative art. The merchant has embarked on a twelfth anecdote, something about fox-hunting in Lower Germany. His narrative style is distinguished by a wildly ungovernable meandering from the proper subject of the tale, until, just when the hapless listeners have all but forgotten the story's aim, the narrative chaotically veers to one side, that is, to the beginning's conclusion, leaving all involved to massage their necks from the rude jolt. This effect had reduced all the merchant's dining company to a dumb stupor, which abruptly broke, like a fouled hypnotic trance, as the merchant tumbled forward into his lamb fricassee with yams in honey-plum brandy glaze garnished with three-times-roasted elephant garlic cloves.

In the third and concluding scene, my father and I have collected the merchant and all of his belongings (sans tapestries, naturally) into his gaudy two-horse coach, and under the milky light of the full moon we are directing it towards a certain high precipice that I know of. My father ruefully shakes his head, the victim of a restless conscience. The coach rattles unsteadily up a steep slope, the merchant dreaming thickly in the back, the ends of his moustache growing longer. At the cliff's edge we rein in the horses, climb off the coach-driver's seat, and begin trying to prod the two horses off the cliff. This is rather sweaty work, as the animals exhibit a reluctance to fall crashing to their death.

I have just recalled that I left the story of my seduction

of the houseguest's wife. We shall leave the coach teetering at the edge of the cliff momentarily, and resume my seduction, before it escapes my attention once more.

Up, up the lovingly-carpeted and oak-bannistered staircase I transported my houseguest's wife, noting her heaving bosom nested like robin's eggs within the infinitude of folds of her crinoline gown. My legs gathered speed as we floated together down a long and tapestried corridor hung with chandeliers. I had planned on carrying her unto my private chambers, but after the taxing length of two corridors I felt my arms becoming numb under the unexpectedly fulsome burden of the deceiving wife. Therefore, I gingerly kicked open the door to an immediately accessible guest room. Inferior ornamentation, but under the circumstances . . .

Mrs. Saltern was clearly struggling to maintain some semblance of composure, vainly battling the ruthless tides of passion that battered her trembling frame. I began reciting a favorite verse into her diamond-studded ear:

> *Magnanimous Despair alone*
> *Could show me so divine a thing*
> *Where feeble hope has presently flown*
> *And proudly flapped its gilded wing . . .*

At this the floodgates tore open. She threw her lily-like limbs about my neck and graced my deep red lips with a kiss, full sweeter than the ripest of plums. One by delicate one I undid the lace clasps decorating her fault-less, custardy bosom, whispering words drenched in honey and imagining her bloated husband's listless state of moronic repose by my fire. Eventually, more of our clothing lay scattered on the Hungarian marble floor than remained yet on our surging bodies. Together we groaned madly from the sheer exertion and, at long last, with a final, desperate squeal, the horses plummeted madly off the cliff, all hooves, legs and manes, the coach and its human cargo not far behind. My father and I fell to the ground, utterly spent by the all-consuming labor, our faces glowing from the primal thrill.

And I wonder if it wasn't some relatives of that mer-chant, having belatedly found out our ingenious scheme of acquiring the tapestries, who set those bloodthirsty hounds loose on my properties? Or perhaps Mr. Saltern, the cuckold, having bumbled across one of my lust-soaked epistles to his charming wife? Or for that matter, Sir Clayridge?

Sir Clayridge, with the very manner in which the tongue is obliged to tap the roof of the mouth with the first syllable of his name, as though in salutation, I am reminded of my eternal contempt. If I am to survive the (steadily approaching) end of this hour, if somehow I may beat off those animals and carry on with my life, I do not feel that fifty years would be sufficient to cool the ardent loathing in my breast for that man. May the Lord forgive the curses and damnation that are to follow.

Sir Clayridge is an uncommonly slim man. Bones jut out sharply from his frame in unnatural places, and his cheeks are sunk in a kind of continual pucker. His arrival is always announced by the eye-clouding stench of the fermented-cabbage gruel he subsists on. He interlards his conversation with aphorisms from the New Testament.

When I first encountered Sir Clayridge I loathed him at once, for all of the above reasons but also because . . . and here I acknowledge a certain helpless irrationality . . . his mother was a Dane. Danes, in one form or another, have been the Waterloo of my ancestors for ages, either through sheer malice, good-natured bungling, wanton alcoholism . . . the causes and narratives are endless and agreeably colorful. Thus, when the properties next to mine were snapped up by the red-faced sack of bones that called himself Sir (Lars) Clayridge, I gnashed my teeth at the thought of the murderous progress of my private installment of the family curse, rendered all the more daemonic by the fact that he was grinning whole-somely at me and inviting me up for an assortment of fish spreads and indigestible black bread. I politely declined and stalked off home to draft a plan.

I began with careful analysis of what I was pitted against. I consulted a volume entitled *On the Danes* by a retired Englishman who had voyaged to the peninsula some sixty years ago.

I was amused to find margin notes in my grandfather's unmistakable limp hand. He had heavily underlined one sentence: "The Danes are enthusiastic, but invariably poor card-players." In the margins, my grandfather had scrawled "Engage Jensen in a round of cards."

I had no way of ascertaining if my grandfather's campaign had been carried out with success, but this seemed as good a place as any to begin. I would invite Clayridge over for a tumbler of brandy, engage him in some gentle cardplaying, and then when he was drunk and vulnerable I would goad him into wagering the deed to his properties.

He came by my properties late, alone, and we greeted each other with an over-familiar warmth, his hand clamping down on mine like the iron jaws of some ravenous hound. I led him in, poured myself a healthy portion of brandy, and was on the brink of pouring him his, when he stopped me apologetically and explained that he forbade himself to drink alcohol, "Blessed are they who hunger and thirst after righteousness" etc., and he would be perfectly content with a rejuvenating draft of fresh apple juice. "Apple juice!?!," I exclaimed in a flurry of rage, looking helplessly at the substantial drink I was clutching. But my refined manners did not permit me to refuse his simple request.

My recollections of the remainder of that evening are a scrappy, piecemeal affair. I remember sitting sullenly in my Louis XIV chair, taking deep quaffs of drink after drink, enduring Clayridge's eternal anecdotes about God knows what. I recall that, fairly swept up in a panic at Clayridge's brazen treachery, I threw the objects lying about on the table to the floor, bellowing "Now we'll have a little game of cards!" and studiously watching for his reaction. His face assumed a leaden composure.

After that there is only fragmentation and humiliation. There is the incident where I drop some of my cards on the floor and hit my head violently on the underside of the table in stooping to pick them up, muttering obscenities all the while. There is the incessant losing, each loss making me more irritable than the one before, the pain sharpened by my opponent's sympathetic smiles. I cannot be sure if I vomited in my own lap.

"Enough!" I eventually cried, tears dribbling down my cheeks and pooling on my outcropping chin, all my wagers lost, reduced to a meager shambles, "I will bet the deed to my properties!" Clayridge raised an inquisitive eyebrow. He stood up from the table and stared down at me, a fallen nobleman. "Perhaps I had better wend my way home," he said flatly. I shook with fury, my eyes flaming like coals, "Leave!" I cried, "May I never again see your cadaverous frame in my home!" He did go, but with one final, inexcusable jab to my pride: he left behind the money he had won from me.

Back I returned to *On the Danes,* though a great deal less incautiously than before. As I flipped the pages with a saliva-moistened finger, I gave special care to information I deemed to have a firm basis in factual observation, versus that founded in speculation and subjectivity. In the former category, my eye fell on a very pertinent detail: "Unlike their jolly neighbors, the Norwegians, who are typified by a passion for the sight of the golden sun ascending over the fjords, the Danes cherish a good, long sleep, and can hardly endure life without it."

Loud construction work, I thought, and first thing in the morning.

Seized by this new plan I tore down to the cellars and hacked apart the plumbing in several out-of-the-way locations with a sturdy axe. To give it a semblance of authenticity, I removed nothing from the cellar beforehand, and a portion of my collection of precious wines were irreparably spoilt by the flooding. I mentally chalked this up as yet another affront Clayridge would have on his conscience, to say nothing of his eternal soul . . . Then I contacted the repairmen, and instructed them to arrive at 5:30 the following morning, and to bring their heaviest tools.

I myself am unaccustomed to the subtle pleasures of the morning. Over a hurried and bloodshot breakfast I spilled coffee across the breadth of a trembling hand, painfully scalding it. I stepped on the tail of my house-coat rushing down the steps to greet the workers, and bloodied my nose falling down.

As the workers hammered apart the stone walkway to gain access to the pipes, I saw a bleary-eyed Clayridge poke his head out of his window to survey the situation. A smile surfaced on my swollen, throbbing lips.

"Very sorry old man," I yelled out, wiping the blood from my close-cropped moustache, "There's been a flood. The workers claim it may be a month or two of work until they have these antique pipes dealt with." My neighbor only groaned in response, fastening his shutters tight.

What then took place was an old-fashioned war of attrition. When he didn't seem near moving out after two weeks of a continuous clanging and bludgeoning of pipes, I hired a second team to come and start building a shed on my prize-winning rose garden, savagely bulldozing the lot of them. This added saw, drill, and a choir of extra garrulous voices to my expanding 5:30 a.m. orchestra. In fact, they worked so effectively that there was nowhere on my properties that their din was incapable of reaching. This was taking its toll on my nerves. I regularly reprimanded the staff for things I had broken myself, if only to find vent for my aggression. But I needed more, I was being prodded to the peripheries of my sanity, and without a blessed moment's reprieve.

Dark, watery circles had bulged out around my cherry-red eyes, and my movements had inherited a dreadful unsteadiness. A dense fog came to dilute the domain of my thoughts. At last came the moment when I cracked. Having been awoken for the fifty-second consecutive morning at the sun's first rays, I grabbed a hunting rifle from the wall, threw open the thick, velvety curtains and aimed directly for a plaid-shirted brute hammering at a pipe and making a sound like a church bell. I have always been a splendid marksman, and my period of unrest in no way impaired this talent. I let fire as the hammer was at the very apogee of its arc, firing my bullet into the base of the worker's skull, that is, where it meets the spine. There was a crisp cracking sound, and time ground its gears to a standstill, the giant hammer in mid-swing, the workmen all half-turned around to look. Then the contents of his head came dribbling out down his neck and his shoulders and his center of gravity vanished and he fell back into the purple clover bespeckled with curious ants and damp with dew.

I must have been a fearful sight, up on my balcony, christened by the first rays of the golden sun, hair tousled from sleep and rifle glistening in my hands. I recall being short of breath though I hadn't been exerting myself. The remaining workers promptly dropped their tools and fled the properties.

My fault, I reasoned, was that my strategies had been

too indirect. My arrangements had been too tenuously linked, and the fabric, in either case, had not held, had frayed. I tossed the worthless *On the Danes* to a watery doom in the still flooded cellar. But on climbing up from the cellar I saw that things had turned awry. A fine mist had entered the properties, and a black mildew could be seen to be gathering around the portraitures of my ancestors. The Argulds were unraveling before my astonished eyes, and moths as big as your fist were chewing terrible holes in them. I ran to beat them away with my scepter, but it rusted and crumbled to dust in my hands. The thick, cloying odor of rotting fruit hung in the air like a pall, like an omen. Rats burrowed their swollen torsos into widening cracks in the walls. I tried to escape the properties but the whole of it, everywhere, wherever I ran was melting like boiling wax, and the very same fata morgana absorbing it all, the dreary mirage of a plain study with no natural light and a writing desk with centuries' worth of life stories crammed in the scratched-up drawers, before the hounds ripped down the doors, the doors which generations of family have not had the foresight to reinforce, the hounds which may in reality be the timid tapping of a priest wanting to offer last rites to a diseased old man, or the dripping of an unmended faucet, or, most grotesque of all possible options, the steady, constant echo of nothing at all.

MR. DELFOUR'S OTHER FILE

The two men walked smoothly, effortlessly even, down the shimmering two-tone corridor, painted chlorine blue and surgical-glove white. One of the men, the one who was markedly taller, walked down the corridor with his hands folded behind his back, in the manner of an intellectual. His eyes won adjectives like "piercing" and "penetrating" from his colleagues, and his hair demonstrated the untamed disarray of a mind that had loftier matters than personal grooming to be attending to. The other man had his arms crossed in front of his chest, the better to stroke his soft chin. Both men had this in common: they wore long white smocks, which had been pressed and bleached until one could not say that they were either eggshell white or lamb's-wool white or even snow white. They were simply white, and both of these men were medical doctors. As they walked they exchanged words, words of such uncommon gravity that they immediately dropped from their orbits about the conversationalists' heads, falling irretrievably out of earshot to everyone who might have desired to hear, to everyone with the important exception of the two doctors themselves. We shall maneuver ourselves gingerly, surreptitiously, ever-nearer to the pair of interlocutors, upsetting a cart of glimmering surgical instruments in our clumsy haste, a prickly bouquet of scalpels, teraphim extirpation pliers and wending hooks clattering upon the waxed floor, dancing chaotically with their reflections. A hallway full of bandaged heads looks up in surprise. The doctors notice nothing, they are far too absorbed in their muttering and chin-tugging. At long last we have gained the necessary proximity to catch the learned dialogue.

"I want you to imagine, Higgins," the tall doctor was saying with an expressive sweep of the hand, "that you are walking along, say, this very corridor. And impossibly enough, what should you come across but a river, very deep and filled with rushing water. The current is swift, indeed." Higgins seemed about to voice a doubt, but this was overruled by an impatient wave of the tall doctor's hand. "In such a predicament you would know full well not to go jumping headlong into that river. But why would you know it, Higgins? Can you answer me that question?"

"Cause and effect," muttered Higgins.

"Ah, yes, our old friends cause and effect, but it is not entirely that simple, is it Higgins? The effect of jumping into the river is only that you fall in. But then the effect of falling in is that you begin to sink, and then the effect of that is sinking entirely, which causes the swallowing of water and the filling of the lungs with water, which leads to . . ."

"Death," said Higgins, stony-faced, "Then we come to death, I believe."

"Very good, Higgins. Now in the unusual case of Mr. . . . (here a rapid flipping through pages on a clipboard) . . . Delfour, this cause and effect system has broken down. When you and I stand by a river, we needn't work our way through the thicket of causes, step by step, we skip straight to the upshot, i.e., drowning and death. But in each individual situation, Mr. . . . Delfour needs to shuffle through all the logical steps. That is to say, the synthesis part of his brain," said the tall doctor, tapping a ball-point pen instructively just above his left ear, "is a wreck. A bona fide cataclysm. But I tell you Higgins, this could be an historical rupture . . ."

An historical rupture! Higgins swooned, only fractionally capable of following his colleague's mountain-goat leaps of deduction.

The two medical professionals found Mr. Delfour's substantial file at the secretary and acquainted themselves with his medical history. The usual stew of ruptures, fractures, fissures and sutures . . . but then something unexpected jumped out at them.

"The patient displays a (. . .) morbid anxiety of (. . .) failure, the dark, heights, fast movement, confined spaces, dogs, and yet has demonstrated (. . .) no associative fear of death."

"Death?" murmured Higgins. It was his second encounter that morning with the word.

"Hmm," considered the tall doctor, wiping his monocle on his smock and bunching up his forehead thoughtfully.

Mr. Delfour himself they found in room 317, in a remote ward of the hospital set aside for "miscellaneous" cases, those patients for whom medical history did not permit easy categorization. He was thickly swathed in bandages and propped up at a jaunty forty-five-degree angle. A ray of sunlight illuminated the room, and the tinny pluck of a guitar came from a small radio. A hanging bed-sheet divided Mr. Delfour from his ward-mate, a man who, to judge by his monotonous groans, must have sustained some sort of head injury. Had either of the two doctors taken the time to go behind the curtain, to step towards the wizened graybeard, whose very appearance suggested superhuman dignity and majesty, had either of them put their ear to the groaning man's colorless lips, they might have perceived that he was stubbornly repeating the word "Yggdrasil" . . . but even then, it is unlikely that anything definite would have been communicated. Both doctors wondered when he might be inhumed.

Higgins officiously approached Mr. Delfour's bedside. His face was a carnival mask of leering sympathy, an expression he had worked on conscientiously, perfected, but then which had over time self-eroded into the present unwitting parody.

"Exactly . . . where does it hurt?" he cooed.

The patient outstretched an uncertain finger and indicated a few sites of particular tenderness at the back end of the cranium and along the strata of the rib cage.

"What . . . exactly . . . has caused this . . . unfortunate mishap, Mr. Delfour?" asked Higgins, selecting each syllable with the utmost care.

"THE FIRST CAUSE?" groaned Mr. Delfour in wide-eyed disbelief and horror. Some bemused chuckling resonated from the ward-mate behind the hanging sheet.

"No, let's not bother with that . . ." intervened the tall doctor, who was routinely made to feel uncomfortable by demonstrations of personal pathologies run amok, "just proceed from the first cause which you vividly remember. State only those things which you have actually experienced." Mr. Delfour seemed to understand

and be reassured by this, and so both doctors took out their notebooks and readied themselves to write.

"In St. Bartholomew's Church, a short stroll down P Street from the market stalls and the children drawing interconnecting networks of squares on the hot pavement, a regional variation on hopscotch which requires twice as many players and, shall we say, a more northern disposition, past the butchers' district, where the meat shops are all decorated with bianca folia blossoms at this time of year, which serve to somewhat obscure the odor of over-ripened meat ferreted out of the trash bins by the neighborhood mongrels, whose ribs, had they been the cheekbones of a lady, might have been described as prominent and whose sudden furies are infamous, past a motley handful of youths with six-dollar haircuts and an unmanageable dread inspired by a first lesson in algebra, delivered in quavering soprano by a Mr. Edilsen Shpilman, who, when confronted by a question from one of his students pertaining to the specific nature of 'x' itself, a question he had neither anticipated nor actually puzzled through clearly in advance, heard his voice relating how in fact 'x' was an abyss, a terrible black space, comparable to the feeling one gets upon waking up in the dead of night with a momentary sense of total disorientation, which is inevitably thereafter replaced with a returning sense of location, but that does not address the dislocation itself, much like we never truly get to the fragile core of 'x'. The boys kick stones at passers-by, who wonder how young people get to be so mean-spirited these days. A little further down P Street there is a medieval brick wall, the other side of which I have never seen, and am never likely to see, and then you are all but there, save for a time-worn stone path flanked with weathered statues depicting scenes of divine intervention . . .

"Thus: In St. Bartholomew's Church, in amongst the gilded clutter and under the mural-painted ceiling criss-crossed with stone buttresses and rafters like you are in the rib-cage of some petrified whale, in the nave to the right of the wall-sized painting of a muscular man hold-ing the slack length of his own skin, a wild grimace on his face not altogether reconcilable with any conventional notion of holy salvation, in just that place I saw . . .

"But what had brought me to the near-deserted and mildewy retreat of St. Bartholomew's Church, you exclaim? Why not the merry pastel colors of the St. Kentigern Mungo, or the richly-illuminated and baroque-inspired St. Turibius of Mogroveio? Or even, come to that, the exquisite harmony of the various tints of blue that lull the faithful in the Church of St. Wmfryd of Wales, patron saint of collapsed lungs, leaving trains and lumps in the throat? I had gone to Bartholomew's to weep. My beloved Nicole, alongside whom I had spent every waking and uxorious moment for seven years and seven months . . . for whom I had removed slivers from tender, coral-red fingers, for whom I had provided weary consolation at 3:00 a.m., whose fingernails I had carefully pared — in short, I had scaled the frontiers of imagination to demonstrate my unconditional and boundless love, no act too vast or too minute, for in the final, celestial scales, every pared fingernail and wayward eyelash is fastidiously marked and weighed.

"Thus, it was unthinkable that anything might draw a shadow between us, but now I have the empirical facts at hand, this bedeviled history has run its course, and now I can only stoke the embers . . ."

"Mr. Delfour, I must insist . . ." began the tall doctor, polishing his monocle on his smock a touch too fastidiously, and stealing a glance at Higgins, who appeared utterly absorbed by the narrative, ". . . that is to say, if you will continue at the present, ambling pace . . . we shall never . . ."

The doctor was abruptly cut off by a howl from behind the sheet, either a cry of stabbing pain or an inhuman sort of laughter. Delfour's ward-mate's files had been lost some time ago, and none of the doctors could recall how long he had been in the hospital, what the exact nature of his ailment was, or even his name. Some doctors feared him, others denied his official existence. Delfour nodded his acknowledgment of the tall doctor's criticism and resumed his story from a different angle.

"I am not sure how to introduce the matter of Mr. Codwell into this already fragmentary affair . . . But it is becoming apparent that I mayn't get much further without his intervention. Suffice to say, when I call to mind Mr. Codwell, it is sitting behind his massive polished desk which offered a matte reflection of his office and, indeed, all available reality by smearing it into a lustreless haze. Mr. Codwell had a small round head, eyes that blinked rapidly, and a well-trimmed, reddish moustache. When he spoke there was evidence of his British ancestry, though he hadn't set foot on the British Isles for twenty-three years. He ran a leather workshop, and on the one occasion that we met for conversation he spoke to me about his father (though this information was unsolicited).

"The elderly Mr. Codwell, Hugh by Christian name, had stumbled into the tanning business quite by chance. He had desperately longed to ask for the hand of Dolly Corshire, who was in every respect the classic Scottish beauty, down to the straw bonnet, and graced with glimmering green eyes to boot, but he had no earnings with which to ratify the request for her hand. So he abandoned his study of mosses, though his botany professors had been unanimous in agreeing that he showed promise, and that the moss analyses that brought regional fame to Clifford MacDuffery would scarcely have been thinkable prior to the innovations developed by Codwell Sr., in favor of an apprenticing appointment in a leather-workers shop. This was work of the most arduous sort, but Codwell bore it out of grim necessity. He estimated that after one and a half years of work he would be in position to overcome the objections of Dolly's parents with a substantial sum. He worked twelve-hour days, under the merciless scrutiny of a Mr. Flaxit, the proprietor of the business and his immediate supervisor. The two men swiftly built up a smoldering hatred for one another, only tempered by the recognition that they were an indispensable commodity to each other.

"It was eight days before the allotted one and a half years, a mere eight days before Codwell Sr. was to take his final payment from Mr. Flaxit, with which he would proudly ride up to Dolly's estate, straight after tendering his formal resignation from the leather business and returning to his first passion, botany, about which he had been having pungent, mossy dreams in the dead of night, sultry, plush dreams of intellectual satiety . . . Eight days preceding this scheduled event, emblazoned in vivid vermilion in his mind's calendar, Dolly came prancing up to him in the street on his way to work. Her face aglow with joy. She cooed out his name and showed him her delicate hand, fluttered it right under his nose, and coiled around one of her fingers was a serpentine ring, the mark of some blackguard . . .

"When I mention that at the stroke of 6:27 that

selfsame evening, an hour at which most are reliving the
tribulations of the bygone day with their rosy-cheeked
families, sitting around the dining-room table as per
age-old custom, perhaps the father indulging in a snifter
of brandy, once in a while can't hurt, when I say that at
that very moment Mr. Flaxit was found run through by
his own awl . . . I may tempt you to draw some unsavory
conclusions, to fill in some intermediate events that are,
strictly speaking, unhistorical. A certain model of pure
historicism cautions us against a steady rearwards
progress from an established event to hastily presup-
posed causes, however much they may satisfy our sense
of narrative justice. To address the particular, we may
speculate that, flung into a searing rage by Dolly's ring,
Codwell Sr. takes momentary flight from his senses,
bids a curt farewell to the faithless woman, walks the
two-and-a-half miles to the leather shop on foot, in the
garish melodrama of a downpour, no less, frightening
children and the elderly en route by the murderousness
of his mien, bellowing curses, kicking cars and streetlamps until, at the scene of his one-and-a-half year
employment, rainwater trickling down his rage-distorted
face and thunder cracking far aloft he throws open the
tannery door with a dramatic sweep of the hand, bellowing "Flaxit!" in a voice that unambiguously proclaims
his volatile mind . . . we could thereafter speculate that
he ruthlessly approaches the aged Mr. Flaxit, gripping

the awl with the initials R(udolph) F carved in the cherry-wood handle, his eyes a pair of red-hot coals . . . But all this would be going too far.

"We shall constrain ourselves to the historical particulars, namely, that Flaxit got his own awl in the back, the police hastened to arrest a shady gentleman who had been skulking in the immediate vicinity and who turned out to have a list of strangulations to his credit, and Flaxit's Thursday afternoon funeral was attended by eleven bereavers, Codwell Sr. inclusive, who thereafter took over the tannery and secured a marriage with a comely distributor that came bi-monthly for deliveries. All these facts Mr. Codwell told me, the junior Mr. Codwell, his eyes moist with tears, on the one occasion I really had the chance to talk with him, whereupon he began telling me his father's story, as though under the influence of a hypnotist, rapidly, breathlessly, unstoppably. When he had finished, his knees buckled slightly, and I had to give him my arm to prop himself up with while he busied himself daubing the sweat off his forehead with a silk handkerchief. It was then that he leant over, motioning my ear closer to his dry lips, and croaked that he had been spending nights with Nicole, my wife, whom you will recall I was uncommonly devoted to. Well, perhaps he did not come right out and say this in so many words, but his meaning, I contend, was transparent . . . or at the very least translucent . . . at any rate, a husband perceives these things intuitively . . . but again, I am skimping on details. I had come to Mr. Codwell's office that day due to an improbable heap of details, strewn about my day with such contrived randomness that I cannot be sure that I haven't merely dreamed it all. Or at least, I might not have been sure, had I not had the confirmation of that brazen confession in his office. Leaving for work this morning I kissed Nicole good-bye, as always, running my fingers down her cheek so as to memorize her softness throughout the day, and as I walked down the street I noted that there was a bit of paper stuck to the sole of my shoe, which I had carried with me from inside of the house. Gingerly unpeeling it, I found it to be a vertically-torn business card, on which was printed

> MR. COD
> HEAD MA
> LEATHER

and on the back, in a gracefully sloping hand,

> *I trust you wi*
> *contact: 42*

"Well, there was probably nothing so terribly mysterious in that on its own, but perhaps the oddity of the surname . . . Mr. Cod, was it! . . . had me perplexed as to what had gotten it onto my shoe. I was meeting a janitor named Eugene MacDavis for breakfast, and thinking about the card occupied me until I arrived at the restaurant.

"Eugene MacDavis was a round man with great, wide-open eyes, and, rightly or wrongly, I felt that I could trust him with the most discreet topics. I liked the way his big, slow head would nod up and down while I talked, a head ready to confirm any statement that my mouth might unpack, but with a touch of old-fashioned sincerity. Eugene MacDavis sat beside me then, sucking on a cigarette with a lazy smile and poking at his scrambled eggs with a fork. That sitting might have carried on indefinitely, punctuated by a coughing diner somewhere behind us and the sing-song click of the overhead fan, but like a fool I started talking.

"'Say, Eugene . . .' I said out of the side of my mouth, warming up to it, 'Do you know how sometimes you have no good cause to think of a thing, there seems no concrete source, but even considering that . . . Well, let's say there are two associative parts of the mind . . . and one of those parts forms associations in a way that I recognize . . . while the other bases associations on more abstract principles, none too clearly defined . . . and when the second part gets, sort of, triggered . . .' What on Earth was I babbling about? Eugene's smile had something off-balance about it. 'Look, Eugene, do you know anything about a Mr. Cod . . .'

"But at this juncture an abrupt spluttering sound made us both turn our heads to look. A man had sprayed soup all across his table, and was putting on his gray trench coat and leaving in a flustered hurry. A rattling of glass signified that he had slammed the door as he went.

"'Sure funny,' drawled Eugene with a shake of the head, 'I've never seen Mr. Codwell beetle off quite like that before.' 'Eureka,' I said monotonously.

"I gathered from Eugene and from the phone book all the rest of the information I required, and then without knowing what I might say, I went to the Codwell leather building at three o'clock that afternoon. But only when Codwell snivelingly divulged the information I have already mentioned, did I realize that I had in fact anticipated it, through that secondary associative function I had struggled to explain to Eugene.

"I am keeping a checklist in my head of things and events that need representation if the ending is to have any chance of making sense to anyone else . . . But put yourself in my place, gentlemen . . . If you were required to explain the building of a lamp to someone who had never seen a light bulb . . . that is . . . If you had to explain a structural critique to someone that had never read the book . . . Bah! Analogy only multiplies my difficulties. So far I have mentioned Dolly, both Codwells, introduced the St. Bartholomew's Church, dabbled in historicism, presented MacDavis and my wife, indicated towards the treachery of the latter . . . I am making fine progress, all things considered, given that I have slept badly and briefly, that my ward-mate was shrieking pseudo-Biblical non sequiturs, in a guttural Scandinavian, no less, for the duration of last night, given that I only dimly recall what started me speaking in the first place. There are only a few more elements to introduce, and then we can return to the ellipses at the start of the narrative.

"Mrs. Alder, widow, had fine motives. Her husband, the deceased Mr. Albert Alder, had been a sound commercial failure. Strong of heart and moral standing, Albert had amounted to nothing in dollars and cents, an imbalance which caused the elderly Mrs. Alder to feel a terrible injustice, which was only one symptom of the lack of righteousness that was the calling card of her era. She chalked this up to Albert's utter disregard for superfluities and extravagances, his overriding belief that people would pierce through the outer ostentations, as some birds do through mollusc shells, to the core, the essence. But people, alas, were not birds, and Albert perished in frustrated misery, nearly penniless, and of a poor man's disease.

"On her deathbed, knowing that her own finale was imminent, wishing to impart something, to preserve some fleeting trace of whatever experience she had husbanded, Mrs. Alder leaned over to her son's ear and croaked 'Spend a little extra on the suit.' Her son, Mortimer Alder, was so much in awe of the papery hand falling limp from his own big hands, her scowling lips and her overall strange ineffability . . . almost transparency . . . that he very nearly overlooked the fact that his mother was uttering her final worldly syllables. When he had taken notice, and when the last, faintly acrid-smelling breath had been expelled from his mother's lungs, he could not help but marvel at the peculiarity of it all.

"Marvel he could, but question was another matter entirely. His eyes glazed with weariness and gloom, he went directly from the deathbed to the tailor's and had himself fitted.

"Four years pass, maybe five. Mortimer secured himself a high-salary position in an office building so tall that the architect was said to have scoffed at the possibility of its execution. His sense of vanity was soothed with every approach to the structure, it was a landmark, he would say, drawing out the first syllable for emphasis, and he had installed himself at its very heart.

"His life had not involved any particular ardor. Buying a suit had given him corporate confidence, which had allowed him to apply for a position and shake hands with a man whose 'means' were abundantly clear from a cursory glance at his office. Mortimer developed a taste for the benefits of the lifestyle, cigars, golf, leather car interiors, and considered himself well removed from whatever vanities had undone his father."

A spluttering caused Mr. Delfour to look up. It was the tall doctor, about to issue a statement of protest. Mr. Delfour raised a hand in acquiescence, as if to indicate "I am just now arriving at the point." The tall doctor tried his best to look only temporarily mollified, recrossed his legs the other way, and waved the patient on with a begrudging snort.

"Mortimer began receiving things in the post. They were always in the same white envelopes marked with no return address, and handwriting so standardized that it might have come from a manual. There was always just Mortimer's name and address and a number, presumably to help him keep track of how many he had received to date.

"Inside the envelopes it was always the same thing. Or nearly. Folded in four, so as to fit inside the standard-size envelopes, would be one faded picture, the scenes slowly, collectively, telling the story of the life of a saint.

"A person less firmly rooted in pragmatics, that is, a person whose mind was liable to get caught by the gills in the net of such a riddle would doubtless have been set awhirl with such curiosities. A different temperament might have spun theories of the probability of x number of misaddressed letters, run through potential senders amongst acquaintances, and eventually, all other recourses bled dry, might have begun dreaming up ghosts, phantoms communicating through imagery in once-weekly correspondence, always Thursday, without fail, phantoms tricking or warning or merely haunting, jamming the gears with their renderings of a halo-capped infant, a wandering youth in torn clothing, a half-visible witness to Christ, perhaps a disciple. Mortimer considered none of these things. He tore open the envelopes with an automatic gesture, glanced at the new picture, and shifted his attention elsewhere. Perhaps he presumed them to be church advertisements.

"The final image was the one most familiar to church-goers: the fully-grown saint being flayed alive, having his skin torn from his body, the viscera laid bare for the viewer most conspicuously. Mortimer stalled on this image. He may have been arrested by its sheer untowardness . . . or perhaps he saw something in it that he recognized, perhaps his mind was deliberating whether or not to plunge into a category of thinking, the symbolic, which it was accustomed to dismissing outright, perhaps it sensed the presence of an intangible precipice which could be stumbled over with a careless footfall.

"In sum, however, there was no result. A thoughtful frown on his face, Mortimer slowly bunched up the saint's image into a tight ball and flicked it out the window.

"The ball of paper fell from the fourth-story apart-ment window, soared through the air, sailed a bit on an easterly breeze, and was piloted into the waiting concave dent at the summit of Mr. Billbent's hat.

"Mr. Billbent was stalking home from the opera in his finest suit (which wasn't so remarkably fine, come to that), his emotions playing havoc inside his triangular skull. He loathed the opera, every sequin, gesture, and sentimental chord moved him to conclude that opera was a vile and anti-intellectual spectacle for people who valued art as an excuse to wear expensive clothing and savor an intermission brandy. The counterfeit emotions stirred not the slightest sensation in his heart, and all the pomp and splendor reminded him of what sheer bombast human pretension could affect, once it had severed the yoke of dignified restraint. And the voices, the voices alternated between a strangled yelp and a canine growl, glissandoing mercilessly across all the intermediate notes. Yet now Billbent was in a bind. He had fallen in love with an opera singer.

"It was quite contrary to his intentions, of course (But what love is not?), yet his heart had convulsed at first sight. He saw her hurrying down a downtown avenue and automatically, absurdly, he swung his body around and followed her. He trailed her over a bridge, lost sight of her at a flower market, found her again dashing past a window filled with pirouetting mannequins, and finally saw her vanish in the back door of the opera house.

"His heart heavy, yet determined, Billbent bought a second-row ticket to the next opera, *Luisa Miller* by the virtueless Verdi. He got into his best suit the following evening, and took a roundabout route to the opera house, so that if any of his colleagues were to see him they would presume him to be bound elsewhere. In his pocket was a newly-acquired pair of opera glasses.

"Billbent sat through the three-hour production with an expression of resolute conviction upon his face. The intermissions he bided in his seat, fending off social advances, smothered in gloomy silence. Then, at long last, his fortitude was rewarded. The woman he loved emerged in the bustle of a chorus scene, in peasant dress, holding a rustic basket of bread perched on her shapely cranium. He was bewitched by her effortless grace, by the gentle undulations of her throat as she sang with the rabble. When she ran off the stage, due to some danger-heralding thump-thumps of the timpani, Billbent collapsed into his seat, his clothing moist with perspiration, his nerves atingle, spent.

"Billbent was snared. From that day forward he was to attend every performance of *Luisa Miller*, three times a week. Sometimes he would fight to abstain, to keep himself about the house, opening up a bit of his favorite writer, David Hume, so as to distract his mind, but his strength of will would inevitably totter and crumble, and the last moment would see him charging off to the opera. His antipathy towards it had not softened one iota, mind . . . he still abhorred everything operatic, cringed at the opening fanfare of the trumpets and then through everything onwards . . . Yet this was but conclusive evidence of the divinity of this woman (whose name he had not learned, was never to learn), that even amidst such filth, in the deepest echelons of the scum of culture, this unprecedented phoenix could rocket forth . . .

"But Billbent came to loathe the torrid depravity of his three-times-weekly routine, and as a consequence, himself. He knew he would forever remain too cowardly to approach his angel after a concert. Self-disgust and shame rose like green bile at the back of his throat, even during the quietest moments. They built up in him like lava, until one night he resolved to endure the helplessness no longer. He left the opera with the intention of, upon returning home, fixing himself a cocktail two parts gin and five parts household bleach.

"On the way home, a crumpled ball of paper landed in his hat and nestled there.

"Mr. Billbent and I were the only two waiting for the 362 bus from the downtown core that evening. I had finally summoned up the strength to go home to my wife after Mr. Codwell's brazen confession, Billbent was going home to drink. We waited some minutes in silence, only the rustle of automobiles slipping by, and then I noticed that the gentleman beside me had something on his hat. Excusing myself, I reached up for it and satisfied my curiosity.

"I have already described the singular picture drawn thereon, but even more extraordinary was the inscription beneath: 'Patron saint of Florentine salt and cheese merchants, and tanners and leather-workers.' I blinked in astonishment, and informed Billbent: 'I have on this very day had difficulty with a leather-worker.' 'Well, then,' he concluded, 'you had best go to St. Bartholomew's Church.'

"And this I did without the slightest delay, by the route already marked out at the start of the narrative. When I arrived it was already late in the evening, but the door was still ajar. I seldom go to churches. Therefore, when I describe the interior of this one as desolate and comfortless, a tomb-like carriage from all that was natural and breathing . . . you must accept that I am unable to state if it was any more or less so than any other church. In I strode, my footsteps making hollow echoes as I went. Bulging, gluttonous cherubs plunged from the pillar-tops, their dusty gilded wings shining back the dim light of candles burning around them, their faces fixed in chimeric leers. Skulls and gravestones encrusted the walls, everywhere streaked with ponderous final salutations in Latin, that most mournful of all available languages. Half-decayed frescoes of martyrs in anguish dominated the walls and the ceiling. I had made it almost to the front altar, unsure of what I might do once I had reached it, when I swiveled, sensing some movement in the nave to my right. It was Codwell. Codwell was slowly moving towards me, a crackle of strange electricity in his eyes, and even before he drew out the antique awl from inside his jacket and raised it above his head like a thunderbolt, even before that I knew his maleficent intentions. 'Codwell!' I howled, and again, 'Codwell!' He peered over his shoulder anxiously, as though urging God to keep out of the forthcoming confrontation. Then he bore down on me. We grappled, I grabbed hold of his thin wrists, the awl sluiced through the air, sometimes stopping only inches from my face. Mad visions swept through my head, I thought he intended to have me skinned; he would jab me to near-death and then peel me of my skin like a ripe banana. I thought that perhaps the story about Codwell, Sr. had been an infamous fairy tale, meant to foreshadow the taking of my life. As we wrestled past a statue of a bishop in supplication, I considered the grotesque possibility that everything . . . the bianca folia blossoms, Dolly, the torn-in-half business card, Albert Alder and *Luisa Miller* had been parts of a careful orchestration, the finale of which was now in frantic culmination. Suddenly, Codwell slipped from my hands. I stopped and looked down. We had struggled to the edge of a trapdoor to a crypt, a trapdoor which had been left open by a monk or a janitor or by God himself, and my adversary had tumbled into the inky depths."

"And in this struggle," ventured Higgins at last, snapping out of it a bit, his fourth notebook filled with rapidly-scribbled notes in a furious hand, his expression pleading, "in this struggle you sustained the injuries which we now see before us?"

"Ho, no, my good fellow, but from these circumstances we can see why I had a natural predisposition to turn away from the St. Bartholomew's Church, a factor whose omission is unthinkable in light of subsequent . . ."

The tall doctor furrowed his brow and considered leaving, but in fact did not move. The simple truth was that he was unable to move, stuck fast in the course of a narrative that was becoming indistinguishable from the cosmos itself. The four men were never to leave that constellation again, the two doctors patiently listening for the cause of injury, Delfour explaining, the voice behind the curtain, whose role in all this is uncertain, and must remain uncertain, groaning or laughing. The ward was cordoned off after a few consecutive weeks of the same, and, in time, the doctors ran out of paper, and thus concluded Mr. Delfour's written file.

GREEN TEA

The first thing you've got to understand is this: as a person, that is to say, due to your very personhood, you are completely in control. Everything you suffer, revel in, or grumble at is infinitely malleable, you are a contortionist or a worm that can suck in its chest until it is paper-thin. As a species, whatever we can imagine we usually get around to creating, sooner or later. Men on the moon, for God's sake. But let me furnish you with a more pedestrian example.

The other day I went into a teahouse, the kind teeming with normal folk who for a lark decide to put on cravats and enormous brooches and talk about art for an afternoon, culling the nearly irretrievable pearls received in grade school literature classes from the cobwebbed recesses of their skulls. Tea steeps, historical facts are exchanged with appreciative mutterings, reconfirmations of confirmed geniuses, "Ah, Yeats! An Irishman, you know . . ." And so on. It was in the very epicenter of this hive of intellectual activity that I placed myself, choosing a chair with my back to Miss Adler, a woman whose letters I had been ignoring for well over three months, a fact which did not daunt her apparent graphomania. She had been pouring her heart out onto my lap weekly, in affected calligraphy, no less, and it was becoming increasingly difficult to divert my wife's attention from those wretched-smelling decorative envelopes that threw the dog into a frenzy of olfactory over-stimulation. She was sitting with an elderly gentleman and kept finding pretexts to fondle his arms or his comic-grotesque jowls, an observation which only justified the seething contempt I already felt for Miss Adler. At any rate, we are coming to a clarification of the point I was making earlier . . . when the waitress arrived, a young woman whose facial tic irritated me to the extreme, I ordered a cup of green tea. I have never enjoyed green tea, not because of some manifest anti-Asiatic prejudice, simply because I have sampled it on numerous occasions, most recently being made to at the apartment of a friend of mine who had recently embarked on a journey of Zen soul exploration or some analogous rubbish, and on every trial my sensitive palette found the aftertaste . . . what the Japanese call the "ghost" of the tea . . . intolerable. And yet, sitting there in the "Winterreisse" tearoom, with a galaxy of teas from which to choose, I selected the green variety. Why? Because as humans we are infinitely capable, as I was saying before, and whereas a wild animal would be instinctively repelled by whatever it was that it had not found to its taste, we as humans consciously choose to defy, indeed to act contrary to our own instincts. It is precisely this that saves us, that elevates us from the primordial morass of bestiality. I listened in on a conversation from a neighboring table.

"I just think that a writer ought to remember his audience, that he's writing for you and me. I'm not talking about the masses now . . . no sir, I don't believe the masses ought to get what they want, not for a minute. But for an educated man like myself . . . Let's be frank, when I'm finished work at the end of the day, what I want is a good story. Don't get me wrong . . ." My interest wavered from the great ox of a man with his very expensive tiepin. My tea arrived. I fear I stared rather too emphatically at the waitress's facial defect, as she was curt, if not hostile with me this time. I lifted up the lid and the vapors caused the corners of my mouth to contract into a grimace of anticipation. I watched it steep for some time — the emeraldness diffusing and rippling outwards from the limp little bag of leaves — and then poured myself a cup. And suddenly I felt aware of the fact that Miss Adler was getting up, she was rising from her chair (I still could not see her, I was facing the other direction), she was patting the bald man on his matte cranium and striding nonchalantly over to the very table which I had hoped would be a private sanctum from the inconsequentialities masquerading as one hundred Zeuses. All around, everywhere, I imagined I heard the arrhythmic clip-clop of Miss Adler's cloven hooves drawing nearer the back of my chair.

"May I join you?"

And then there she was in reality, standing right before me, her hand perched meaningfully on the chair across from mine, as though on the verge of sliding it out and slithering onto it. Before answering I put some sugar into my tea. Take my word, I did not relish the thought of a few hours' captivity *sans murs, avec la femme intolerable.* And yet, as I was saying, I felt compelled that day to exercise my infinite capability, my ability to make any decision regardless of its apparent vileness. A rodent would retreat in horror from a parasitical worm, I told myself, but I would not be so bullied by Miss Adler. I made a little gesture with a hand, discreetly signifying that she could seat herself if she liked. With a knowing smile (but knowing what?) she sat herself down. There was then an expectant silence, not at all the kind of silence that one wants to do away with, that makes the involved parties babble convictionless nonsense for the sake of speaking, but rather the anticipatory silence that one knows will eventually be ruined by some pedantic comment, and so one struggles to hold on to it for as long as one can, smothering oneself in the perfect lack for as long as is socially feasible. There was something undeniably piggish in that smile of hers.

"I didn't expect to see you here."

You see, as soon as the mouth opens, clichés start spilling out like sludge from an unblocked pipe.

"I'm enjoying a cup of tea."

And as if to confirm my statement I lifted the still-steaming cup to my lips and took a long slurp, an act which prompted my face to wince horribly. Miss Adler tittered into her lace-lined handkerchief, thinking that I was trying to be quaintly amusing. She leaned forward onto the table in such a way that she exposed the contours of her bespotted bosom. Her lips pursed themselves into an exaggerated pout.

"You haven't been writing to your *chere amie* for some time," she crooned, maintaining her foul habit of sprinkling her conversation with French phrases, despite her almost absolute ignorance of the language, "I was starting to become . . ." (here she adjusted her bra straps in what might have been a poorly executed gesture of seduction, unless I miss my guess) . . . "worried. That you were trying to tell me something."

The truth of the matter is that "indifference" does not for all intents and purposes exist in the popular lexicon. In not reacting, one reacts.

"No, I wasn't," I mumbled almost inaudibly.

"Well, good."

There was that knowing smile again. It occurred to me that it was entirely synthetic, that it did not reflect anything except knowingness, hoping to affect a confirmation of whatever indecencies might be fluttering about in my mind without knowing what they were, or indeed, if they even existed. It seemed to me the height of absurdity, communicating gestures that signaled only themselves. I started to feel vaguely pathetic participating in this entire charade. A new, gloomy silence had settled over our table like the news of a death and neither of us knew quite what to do. So I slid my arm under the table and put my hand on the upper part of one of her stockinged legs. Let me assert: I love my wife, completely, in a way that annihilates doubt. But do I need to explain myself for a third time? After the matter of the green tea . . . and the invitation to sit down . . . am I required to elaborate any further? Will you not concede that I was just seeing this thing out to its logical conclusion? My wife and I had been almost eleven years together, and scarcely a quarrel had arisen between us. I didn't even find Miss Adler physically alluring: she was over-skinny, over-perfumed, overbearing . . . her eyelids looked as though they were conspiring to push the bulging jelly of her eyeballs out from their sockets. Her voice brought to my mind a particularly vindictive schoolmarm (fifth grade, history I believe). And yet . . . there I was, lingering with my obscene, under-the-table gesture. A nod of the head and we were off.

I always put the trousers on before the socks. I suppose at one time I had the idea I looked preposterous strolling about in only my underwear and socks, and so I made it a rule to put on the trousers first, despite the fact that I no longer have any delusions of looking less than absurd when undressed. It was only mid-afternoon, and there I was crawling out of bed for the second time. Miss Adler still lay under the covers, again smiling that knowing smile, and I caught myself wondering if this time there might not actually be some knowledge behind it. I gave her a kiss on the forehead before leaving. The aftertaste of the green tea still lingered nauseatingly on the back of my tongue. I took a little mouthwash and everything was back to normal.

THE PALACE

*For beauty is a disease, as my father maintained; it is
the result of a mysterious infection, a dark forerunner of
decomposition, which rises from the depth of perfection
and is saluted by perfection with signs of the deepest bliss.*
                                    Bruno Schulz, "A Second Fall"

In the Palace, there is a temporary relief from conventional impositions of cause and effect. A crystal decanter topples from a six-foot high shelf, breaking into pieces and taking with it the last traces of an artisan from Charbonne who slept as an inferno drew the strings of an endless black curtain. The lord does not query the butlers to find one that may have nudged it with his elbow; nor does he beat the cats for good measure; nor does he shake his fist at the mischievous caprices of the wind for having placed a gust at such an unlikely slope. But the kitchen may switch to a darker rye bread, or the dock may be cleared of its lop-sided ducks, or the gardener may come to smile less toothily.

In the Palace we have an ideal show of symmetry. For

each room four walls, and a floor opposite its ceiling. If a bright cloud drifts over the pond, an equal appears on the pond's still surface. If a rowboat is tied to the dock at the back, a car is parked in the front driveway. If the lord's daughter weeps in the scullery, the sewing-maid is obliged to sing a folk melody. If the young master of the house steals chocolate from the pantry, his shadow is boxed up and stored in the attic with the photographs and assorted memorabilia.

Each season the Palace is painted a new color. There are four colors to choose from. There is an accepted method of deciding which color to paint next. If we are in Winter, moving towards Spring, it is clearly futile to repeat Winter's color. Nor are we ready to once more take up Autumn's color, so freshly covered by Winter. Taking last year's Spring color would reduce the Palace to the monotony of seasonal and cyclical routine. Therefore, only Summer's color is feasible and proper. The four colors are: auburn, indigo, cream, wine/burgundy.

The Palace's walls appear to slant dangerously outward but they are in fact impeccably straight. The floor, too, appears to be at an incline, and yet one may affirm its flatness by placing a ball on it and watching the ball remain motionless. An architectural conundrum: the precise ninety-degree angle fools the eye and appears to incline terribly through its excessive perfection. Just as a wall near collapse may appear exactly upright when seen in one's periphery.

An Abridged Architectural History

In 1479 Baron von Kaldrenson, having made a considerable fortune in some enterprise not recorded in any logbook (!), bought a piece of land sight unseen on which he intended to build his own palace to carefully arranged specifications. He arrived to find the plot a ghastly mire, totally unsuitable for building upon. He very nearly threw his blueprints into the murky depths, to the mocking approval of the local villagers (the opportunity to scoff at an aristocrat did not come along every day). Enraged, von Kaldrenson vowed to erect his extravagant palace on the mire at quote any expense endquote. Construction progressed slowly. Swarms of nibbling insects irritated the workers and spread disease. The mire needed draining bi-weekly. Plants carefully uprooted grew back at remarkable speed. The roads for transporting materials were plagued by potholes, wolves and bandits. The construction team was rotated every five months or so owing to low morale and serial nightmares while sleeping on the grounds. In six years, the skeleton had been completed. After nine and a half, the baron was able to move into the Palace.

The swamp, however, would not be defeated. A thin and gelatinous mud oozed persistently between the cracks in the walls and floors, soiling the imported fineries. Insects made nests in the larder and poisoned the meats. Worst of all was the smell that none of the occupants ever reported growing accustomed to, a strangling stench that could be felt in every room at every time of day or year. It was variously described as "verminous," "intolerable," "suffocating," and perhaps most insightfully, "the terrible odor of moldering humanity." After seven months the baron had reached his wit's end and fled, complaining of chronic headaches and tremors. Half of his kitchen staff had already been sent to an asylum with undocumented afflictions.

Somehow, von Kaldrenson persisted. Brick by brick he had his Palace meticulously disassembled and then transported to a green vale with billowing clouds and noted for the sweetness of its air. The process lasted a mere four years, and was feverishly overseen by the baron, whose temperament improved monthly after being removed from his ordeal. It was a fully recovered von Kaldrenson, then, who puffed out his substantial chest (regional sparring champion 1477) and walked into his rebuilt Palace to find the revolting smell somehow intact, transported with the very stones. The baron tore out his hair and abandoned the place, never to return.

In the Palace, all the portals are one-way. If a person should enter the Palace through the front doors, he is only free to exit through the rear. Naturally, if he enters through the rear, it follows that he exits through the front. Therefore people move through the Palace as though being driven by invisible currents, by tides that are at liberty to stall, but not draw back. Every maneuver is irretrievable. I know of one case in the late 17th century where an incautious stablehand opened the front door halfway as though to enter, but then thought better of it, walked around the Palace to change his boots around back, and then entered through the back door. In this way he trapped himself, and was unable to leave the Palace by either exit (for they were both of them entrances). He needed to be lowered out of a second-story window with a rope tied around his heel, and proved so unsettled by the incident that he thereafter quit the properties.

In 1628 the renowned occultist Johannes Kepler published a seldom cited tract (last reprinting under the title "Traktat Samowładzy Pałacu," Wrocław 1907) on the autonomy of the Palace. In a treatise seemingly altogether divorced from his normal preoccupation with mysticism, Kepler soberly affirms that the genius of the Palace lies in its unanimous non-adherence. To briefly quote: "When we speak of the Palace, what concerns us is the capturing of a certain whimsicality . . . if we think we recognize certain principles of architecture or historical allusions in the various arcs and portals, we would do best not to see these as concessions or borders, but as necessary. For the Palace, being absolute, must contain everything." Kepler's hastily prepared thesis (he was in the advanced stages of consumption) has not received any serious review.

During a two-week period of relentless rainstorm, the lord recorded in his journal that the Palace "felt sad."

The bookshelves of the Palace library all face towards the East, in accordance with Lao-tzu's principle that the books of a house ought to be consecrated daily with the first rays of the rising sun. Over time this had the unanticipated effect of bleaching all the spines, so that a blind man needed to be hired to act as librarian, "reading" the titles on the spines with his fingers.

An Abridged Architectural History (II)

Being short of money and hot-blooded by nature, Baron von Kaldrenson's only nephew lost the Palace in a single round of cards (Method: Scopa. Error: a clear reluctance to play the game aggressively, as is required. Outcome: Drunken disbelief and the pounding of his ham-like fists on the table). His shrewd opponent, Signor di Scarafaggio, smirkingly scooped up the deed and moved his things to the Palace that very week, all the while twirling the corners of his extensive moustache. Von Kaldrenson's nephew spent the next undetermined period drunkenly mourning his loss in public, a period concluded by his release from prison seven months later. It would seem that a single thought occupied his mind at this point, if we may judge by extant fragments of his journals and the feverishly written letters to his bedridden mother: how to dispatch the Signor.

Whether the nephew's fixation started within the Palace, that is to say, whether the origin of the brain fever lay within the substance of the loss of the Palace and then spread outward from that impossible coordinate multiplicitously, but then narrowing and ultimately focusing on Signor di Scarafaggio . . . this cannot be proved. Nor can the Palace be outright dismissed, for it was after all to that place that the nephew returned with a longish dagger, mother-of-pearl carved into the shape of a mule inlaid into its handle, tucked under his belt. His last journal entry pithily summarizes the departure as follows:

"Any last doubts have vanished. Surely the most persistent voice is God's?"

Meteorological records for that day report violent rains and hard winds. The nephew arrived at the Palace grounds at 19:42, a fact recorded by the dutiful doorman. His clothing was generously dappled with mud, his jacket torn, his hair oddly askew, and his eyes searing with a barely-brooked passion. In short, the appearance of a madman. He was denied entrance, and warned amid his two-fisted thumping on the door that the authorities would be summoned unless he cleared off. Bellowing wildly, the nephew of Baron von Kaldrenson climbed up some sturdy vines towards a third-story window, lost his footing on the wet brick, and tumbled to his death. His face, contorted though it was by an anguished grimace, was dimly recalled by the Signor, and his body was buried behind the Palace's shed.

The grounds of the Palace are a fixed area. This does not refer to the banalities of property ownership, but rather to what clemency might lead us to describe as the personal effects of the Palace . . . otherwise, the baggage. But to the cagey observer, the grounds may seem only to direct focus to the Palace. The paths show pretensions of meandering, yet inevitably slant towards the center, reaching their appointed climaxes at the front doors. The trees thin in anticipation. The heads of all the flowers are turned Palaceward.

In the 19th century, the Palace was analogized as follows: the Palace is to conventional architecture as the operatic voice is to everyday speech. This would seem to suggest that the Palace is inflated, anachronistic, or unnatural . . . but all of these conclusions suffer from being too literal. It is true that the Palace is a form of conscious development, but as such, may not be characterized until it is obsolete.

There are those who, while smiling indulgently from under their moustaches at the Baron von Kaldrenson story, cannot help but find it a shade too clever. There are those who would maintain that these origins have been entirely fabricated. That the Palace in its autonomy must a priori have created itself as well. A now-remote center point that pulled itself outwards through some kind of immeasurable will. The issue is confused by the inescapable fact that all evidence of the Kaldrenson family (assorted documents, portraits, signed letters, a half-finished poem in the epic style by the nephew, the baron's personal seal), Signor di Scarafaggio, his entourage, and even Miss Druthers, said to have had countless social connections and half-hearted intimacies, has been found only in the Palace or on its properties. The numerous attempts to isolate "extra-Palatial" evidence of these historical personages, initiated in the main by historians reluctant to allow the so-called frivolities of philosophy into their sober arena, have proved fruitless.

Onto the tiny footbridge leading over the artificial pond are carved numerous representations of a mule or an ass. Either side of this bridge gently directs the stroller to the Palace.

An Abridged Architectural History (III)

Even the Palace's normally exhaustive records largely plead ignorance regarding the final two years of Signor di Scarafaggio's residence at the Palace. It is known that before that, he had feverishly built extensions onto the Palace, with seeming disregard for the unities of style, shape and form. Here he would erect an outcropping with High Renaissance flourishes, there a Turkish-inspired tower jutting wildly from the roof. History, however, has revealed a method to this incoherency, shown accusations of thoughtlessness to merely not grasp a thought of extraordinary scope and complexity. The Palace superseded collage in the singularity of its wholeness.

Of those last two years only a pair of details are known. Firstly, that a British widow by the name of Miss Druthers had come to live at the Palace. Secondly, that the Signor died quickly and violently, gouged twelve times by his own blade. The conclusion of suicide reached by officials in charge of the case is today regarded as rather unsatisfactory by the majority of historians. "A man who has just dealt himself eleven mortal wounds," sums up one critic, "seldom has the strength to deliver a twelfth."

Under the subsequent occupancy (we demure from the term "possession") of Miss Druthers the Palace acquired a wholly different complexion. The staff was forever suffering from dizzy spells and fatigue. The head butler, who had served for thirty years in the Palace, vanished for a period of two and a half days. When he staggered into the drawing room after this time, his head was bruised and puffy and he was able only to explain that he had "gotten lost." A thick layer of snow generally covered the Palace. Miss Druthers' diary finds her wondering at the shortness of her memory and that of the other occupants of the Palace, as though "Ideas had become so airy that one could scarcely keep one's grasp of them for a moment before they dissipated entirely."

Miss Druthers' time at the Palace concluded as mysteriously as it had begun. Her diary, the last existing record of her final year, drifts from semi-coherency to metaphysics to what can only be described as lunacy. "Daily I concentrate," she writes, "I pool my resources to separate what is mine, the interior, from all that is the Palace . . . with each passing day this becomes more difficult."

If I were to try to write about the Palace I would surely fail. I would get lost amidst comparisons, hopelessly entangled in a language ill-equipped for uncertainties. I might try to employ paradoxes, with the dim hope that the right dialectic might bubble to the surface. I might appeal to the authorities or great thinkers to lend weight to my simple observations. Only as a last resort would I plead.

I should prefer the task of describing the Cataclysm, of assessing the boundaries of human ingenuity, of discovering a new continent to that of writing about the Palace. I should prefer to be asked to write the libretto to Schubert's "Trio in Es-Dur op.100," or to create an archetype.

In the den of the Palace are drawers filled with unfinished and only hastily labeled architectural plans, seeming to allude to constructions that are, by all appearances, unrealizable. More colorful suppositions have included that these plans can only be reflections of the future of the Palace, somehow located in the present day. Or others, that the plans are already inclusive in the Palace but simply buried under a more primitive façade.

To speak of the motives of the Palace is tantamount to admitting to its deeper consciousness. Yet how can we omit them, when the motives seem so plain, so evident? For the Palace, nothing can be said to exist outside of its notion of self . . . and all of its historical personae remain in its archives insofar as they bear relation, or pertain to it. Its motives, then, can only be those of self-interest. Outside of this duty to itself, the Palace stops existing.

Only as a last resort would I plead. Ladies and gentlemen of the Assembly! I have thrown myself on my knees before you, lifting my trembling arms up to your remote heights, palms open wide! I have played my final card before you, it lies at your feet gasping terribly like a beached carp! And what if, you might ask, the Palace should not exist at all but for my poor summary? If, however unthinkably, the flawed reflection should out-live its source?

If I were to try to write about the Palace, I would surely fail.

THE CORRIDOR

*What was most surprising was that the corridor began
from his head, i.e., it was just an endless continuation of
his head, the sinciput of which suddenly opened up into an
immeasurable expanse.*

Andrei Bely, *Petersburg*

Ummm . . . lugubriously . . . I raised myself . . . from
the so-to-speak couch. My eyes were operating jerkily,
lacking in grace and feeling as though filled with water,
trying to follow the movements of some maddened spider which . . . strictly speaking . . . may or may not have
actually existed.

Which amounts to the intangible side of things.

Tangibly speaking, in my left hand was a packet of
cigarettes in that uncomfortable area between four and
six remaining: too many to consider buying another
pack, too few to get through the evening. Wincing, I
shook out another.

If I shy from the tangibilities, if I demure and turn a
shade crimson, it is because I gnash my teeth in writing

of them. I count reportage among the most futile of activities (see also: elaborate cooking, sport of any kind, prize-winning novels, etc.); I rush through it or usually alter it from spite.

Ummm . . . lugubriously . . . I raised myself . . . from the so-to-speak couch.

Today I have awoken with a steadily deepening sense of the approach of the absolute, like a shimmering comet from a remote corner of the sky or a letter incorrectly sent to my address. I feel as though everything is an indication, gesturing towards something so vague and incredible that it could only be gestured towards. And that, moreover, the gestures are accumulating, building architectures that claw horribly at the heavens, and that perhaps with agonizing soonness . . .

My fingers lumbered stupidly through a matchbox.

. . . perhaps with agonizing soonness reality would be altered so slightly that one will wonder if one hasn't fallen victim to an endless series of false perceptions, wherein understandings become open-ended questions, everything is undermined, a triumph of sleight of hand.

I record the following on the sideways chance that something terrible should befall the protagonist (i.e., myself) this evening, to stand as a recollection and a direction or scent for the bloodhounds.

Waiting for me this morning was a small brown parcel, and as you might anticipate, I seldom get mail. Thus

I was not surprised at the information that the package was not addressed to myself but rather the Spaniard down the hall. My communications with Mr. Alfau had dwindled from initial courtesy to scarcely visible gestures of recognition, the slightest curl of the corners of the lips into a taut smile. For my part, I freely concede that I took an appalled fascination with the thickets of hair spread over the backs of his hands and onto the first set of knuckles, and perhaps he found my lavished and indiscreet attentions somewhat wanting in tact. I was about to put on my shoes, place the thing on his door-mat, ring the bell, and then slip back into my flat like a wraith, when I noticed that the return address was writ-ten in Arabic script. This curiosity conspired with the ingenuity of the wrapping to cause me to stay a moment longer.

The theorist A. Scott Thomas in his *Elements of Theatre* proposed that "All tragedy can be traced back to a single moment of indecision." He goes on to assert that this uncertainty signals to the audience the possibility of an alternative course of events ("If only he hadn't drunk the wine!" etc.), and it is this, rather than such-and-such consequences, that is the proper embryo of tragedy.

So I paused a moment staring at my shoes, wonder-ing if perhaps cosmic significance might be attributed to this package, in my flat, on this very day . . . And then I was on my bed, parcel squarely on my lap, staring at the

Arabic characters as though with sufficient concentration they might untangle themselves and reassemble into recognizable letters. The stamps depicted a man about to have his head lopped off by some manner of Middle-Eastern sword, the eyes of the executioner glaring out to meet those of the living mail recipient, as though threatening his audience rather than his victim. No doubt about it, the parcel would have to be delicately opened, and then rewrapped in the same manner as before.

My fingers work bullishly when I am concentrating on their actions with all my might. Ordinary procedures are rendered into colossal hardships or miniature vaudeville routines. To make matters worse, the package had been wrapped using the Indian paper trick.

Had I full reign of my senses, I would have recognized the trick straight away and taken the necessary precautions. But alas, only when the wrappings fell apart in my hands with miraculous ease, as if through some enchantment, only then did I fully grasp my dilemma. I well knew that to wrap the package in the same manner would require a detailed manual with illustrations. Irritated, I turned my attention to the contents.

I was holding a small ivory box. On the lid and along the sides were friezes depicting the story of a martyr. The first three frames illustrated his arrest, hands bound behind his back and slung over a tiger, men with long and exotic weapons on either side. The following three showed the torture of our hero, variously suspended by hooks or flagellated by a one-dimensional captor or being covered in spiders. Frames seven through nine were of the procession, with all the pomp and show of an old-fashioned execution, musicians, men on horseback, costumed soldiers. When I turned the box finally to see the concluding frame, to my disappointment I found it to be scratched out.

I went through the series again, noticing aspects I had overlooked the first time . . . a monkey crouched amidst the branches of a bent tree, a traitorous grin on the face of one of the guards, a shadow belonging to someone lurking outside the frame of the picture. No, I had "read" it correctly . . . my second effort also ended in frustration by the ruined tenth image. My patience now exhausted, I undid the latch and flipped open the top.

To this moment I maintain the credibility of my senses in what was only a brief glimpse into the darkened interior of a box. When one starts to question one's senses it is a slippery slope, invariably resolving with our old friend madness, poised like an eager father ready to catch his child at the bottom of a playground slide, arms wide open and head nodding reassuringly. Inside the box I caught a glimpse of a statuette of myself. The length of the arms, the part of the hair, the gentle slope of the spine, even the ill-fitting clothing (nearly my entire closet had once been my father's, now dead, but a considerable-sized man in his youth) were unmistakable gestures towards a quite perfect replica of the protagonist. All this might have been alarming enough in itself, but what was more, my, or rather the statuette's face was frozen in an expression of utter horror. The implication was unambiguous enough . . . the sculptor had depicted a man staring into the face of certain death. My hands began trembling wildly, and I began trying to rewrap the loathsome object, as though by returning it to its one-time state of being blissfully unknown to me, I could come to believe that I had never seen it. This circuitous and deeply flawed logic was further thwarted by my inability to execute the elaborate folds of the original packaging. In the midst of my struggles and contortions the doorbell rang.

I trust that you will show a bit of understanding when I tell you that I very nearly dropped the package from fright. At the best of times I anticipate the inevitability of a visitor with a kind of numbing dread. Moreover, I had already been worked into a state of semi-panic deciphering the machinations of the paper trick. I opened the drawer of my nightstand and threw it all in, slamming the drawer shut. I only had time to wonder about the nature of the cracking noise from within before running over to the door.

My door is equipped with a tiny window through

which, if one's eye is pressed so that it nearly touches the glass, the whole of the visitor can be viewed with certain distortions. This I consulted before opening the latch, to see the slender frame of my neighbor, Mr. Alfau.

At that point the mains pipe burst somewhere in the back of the protagonist's skull. I did not want to believe in any of the outright lunacy that was filling my head, but I had faith in cause and effect, that Mr. Alfau was standing in front of my door dressed in a light-colored Mediterranean suit and fiddling anxiously with his cuff links for a reason . . . and whether this second invasion into my privacy proved innocent or not, perhaps the process had to be seen through . . .

I lifted the latch and gave Mr. Alfau my most inviting expression, something between a grimace and a look of quaint surprise. He brushed past me and, searching in vain for a chair, sat himself at the foot of my bed, producing some foreign brand of tobacco and lighting it.

"I . . . have found . . ." he began with terrible slowness, somnambulently almost, ". . . a letter addressed . . . to you . . . in my postbox." He narrowed his eyes and leveled his gaze at me, removing a small envelope from his breast pocket. He continued turning the letter about in his hands as blue-gray strands of smoke escaped his mouth, tailoring intangible fabrics in the air. ". . . And I know that sometimes . . . it happens . . . that mail is . . . switched, by mistake."

A moment elapsed with syrupy reluctance and I felt certain that the lights dimmed for an instant.

"So I thought I would . . . stop by . . . and perhaps you have something . . . a letter, a package . . . for me." It took every iota of my concentration to bury the expression of alarm that was struggling to affix itself to my features, replacing it with one of benign impatience.

"I'm sorry, but there hasn't been . . . a letter," I managed, unintentionally parroting his pace.

He stared at me gravely for an instant.

"A pity . . . a great pity . . . But then my aunt used to warn me of expectations, of effects and the randomness of causes, she was a tall and slender woman with a wide mouth, my aunt, and her bearing . . . God knows what is really being alluded to by this word, but her bearing was one of royalty, an impression that was only confirmed by the excesses of her villa . . . peacocks in the garden, the Pre-Raphaelite decadence of pastry each afternoon without exception, engraved silver trays bearing puffs bursting with pink cream, for every lady a lace-trimmed . . ." . . . but alas, at this point Mr. Alfau's droning voice began fading into the background, the very mention of cumulonimbus pink cream having sent me into reveries of my own, whereupon as a six-year-old boy my parents had taken to regular public rows and to distract me from the goings-on they would stop by a bakery, their faces burning red from the exertion of maintaining their temporary truce, and buy me a treat while they stepped outside to yell. I vividly recall a particular fluffy pink confection, which I ate with my fingers while watching the gesticulations of my maddened parents on the pavement outside, my mother's enormous teeth flashing as she yelled, my father betraying no evidence of emotion save the modest wrinkling of his forehead. What followed was an excerpt from a sentimental film. The baker, a mountain of a man in a butter-smeared apron, clearly saw the truth of my predicament and came out from behind the illuminated glass case overspilling with éclairs and chocolate-ensconced caramel-cluster dandies in order to give me a hug. I wept for maybe a minute, my arms and tear-soaked face enveloped in the sticky folds of the baker's monstrous frame, my nostrils filled with his impossibly sticky perfumes. My parents never caught a glimpse of that hug, but the baker gave me a little decorative marzipan dragon, which for reasons best left unexamined remains on my bookshelf today. It suddenly struck me that Mr. Alfau was still prattling on.

". . . at which point the package was shoved rather too hastily into a drawer, as a terrible cracking noise could be heard from within."

My mind struggled to find a context for this line, feeling as though it were inside of a great hole, and dirt were raining down on it. Mr. Alfau had simply stopped talking, contenting himself with the languid lighting of a second cigarette, his eyes studying my face. I refused to rule out the possibility, however slight, of an accumulation of coincidences . . . I cursed myself for not having paid attention to his story . . . if only . . . I could see that I was left with a single recourse, however hateful and ghastly that it was.

"Please . . . continue. What happened after that, Mr. Alfau?"

"I'm very glad that you asked . . . because here is where the story takes on a very peculiar character, indeed."

The cocky Spaniard took a long, self-satisfied suck from his cigarette, his scarlet lips performing ugly and perfidious contortions on the platform of his face.

"It happens that inside the cut glass of the package's contents was a tiny and extremely poisonous spider. The spider slipped through the cracks of the drawer like a shadow and crawled in between the toes of the poor fellow as he slept that night. His body was found only three days later by a concerned neighbor who had stopped seeing him in the corridor between apartments."

I feel fairly certain that my face involuntarily blanched at this point, my circulation becoming hurried and irregular. "That's a nightmare," I choked out at last. "Yes . . ." agreed Mr. Alfau almost nonchalantly, "My aunt was stunned for weeks . . . we couldn't feed her anything but creamed soups, and even those with great difficulty."

Mr. Alfau ventured a chuckle at this, which I parroted unconvincingly. He grimaced slightly.

"Well, I'll leave you, then. Forgive me for having taken your time." And with that he abruptly picked himself up, swung open the door and left, leaving me with a room full of horrors, imagined or otherwise, and without even giving me the letter he had brought. Exhausted to the point of indifference as to whether or not I'd been given a prophecy, I fell into a heavy afternoon sleep, though notably with my shoes on.

THE GALLOWS

But there was another deeper reason, not too clear as yet, a promise of another life, all shining and colourful, which was erasing the memory of the old one.

Luigi Pirandello, "The Soft Touch of Grass"

Dalia, if right now I could compose a love letter to you I would have trouble beginning for the trembling of my fingers: I would start gingerly, not with a recapitulation of your odd beauty (though you are all of that) in the high Renaissance style, but rather incomplete sentences and approximations of thoughts, in the same way that I am only a beginning or a tentative suggestion of something in your absence . . . I would follow that with a list of words I've been reserving for use with regards to you — sheer, utter, insatiable, remote . . . I would resolve with a moan or a gasp or a sigh or whichever utterance seemingly befits that moment of boundless release . . . Oh, Dalia, if right now I could compose a love letter for you it could say anything at all, but it would have to include five words: "I have never been so."

Like a hopeless naif, I treated that morning quite like any other, eyes drowsily scanning the daily news items while the hands and mouth saw to eating. I had for some time suspected that my role was overstepping its proper boundaries. At one time I had been content to be a waiter for a full eight hours, and then upon returning home I would feel the weight of this act drop from my shoulders like a heavy satin cape. But shortly the hemispheres started blurring. I would come home and prepare my own food with idiotic flourishes. I started being overly accommodating with my friends, many of whom stopped associating with me. I would apologize for things that were not my fault.

I could sense this dreary progress of this transformation, but was powerless to stop it. It was as though I were hovering somewhere above my own head, watching myself from afar, only able to stare in mute horror at my meticulous polishing of my own silverware, the way I'd breathe into and then wipe my own wineglass with the cloth that was still — for some inexplicable reason — slung under my belt. At any rate, that morning was the most serious yet. I went so far as to place on the table cutlery that I knew I would not use.

I set out for work feeling distracted and unsettled. To what extent would my role as a waiter dare to encroach upon my actual life? Would I have to consciously set rules for myself when not at the restaurant? And if so, how could I think of that as a natural life? For the time being, at least, I felt assured that "I" was not a "waiter." This whole tangle of nonsense distracted me to such a degree that I nearly missed my stop.

My feet automatically knew the way from the All Saints' Place tram station to the Restaurant. To ward off a ticklish breeze, I turned up the collar of my jacket. Winter won't be long in coming, I thought.

"Winter won't be long," announced the head waiter, ostensibly to me, as I pushed open the heavy glass doors of the Restaurant. I shivered audibly as a form of reply, taking off my overcoat in the always-temperate sanctuary of the Restaurant. "Roy!" cried the head waiter so loudly and abruptly that I nearly jumped, "Where is your bow tie?" A glance down at my neck confirmed the unthinkable . . . my morning state of befuddlement had caused me to forget it. My hands grasped in agony at the barren and stiffened collar. "I will run out and buy another," I heard my voice volunteer, somehow steadfast and confident, as though a new bow tie weren't the better part of a day's wages.

"I'm giving you fifteen minutes."

Back on the morning streets, I was gripped by an attack of the nerves. I'd no idea where to find a bow tie so early in the morning, particularly one that would match my upper-middle-class suit. The streets led me in circles, forming baffling patterns and shifting their cobblestones under my very feet. At last my eye caught a weathered sign flapping mournfully over a darkened window, and reading The Bow Tie Co. My heart leapt at the sudden and unexpected good fortune. A woman dressed entirely in shades of brown was unfastening the lock to the shop with great effort.

I stood and watched her exertions, the little clock in my mind rushing ever more speedily to the gallows of fifteen elapsed minutes. Shortly, the anguish became unendurable.

"Look, let me help you with that." I blurted, perhaps a little too severely under the circumstances. The young woman let go of the keys and stood aside as I tried my hand at it, taking a sideways glance at her face. Something in her eyes at that moment overwhelmed me with its gentle and so very human beauty. So much so that my hands' activities simply stopped dead, and a strange glow of absolution fell over my face. I was only shaken out of this when I caught a glimpse of my absurdly gaping reflection in the windowpane, shook my head in cartoon embarrassment, and applied myself with redoubled diligence to the matter of the bolt. As I grappled with it, a lot of rubbish came spilling out from between my frozen lips.

"I'm a waiter you see and I've left my bow tie at home and the head waiter who even under normal circumstances can't be depended on to be reasonable has given me fifteen minutes to find a bow tie to match the suit I've got on and though I've been having quite serious reservations of what we might call a philosophical nature about carrying on with this line of work this is hardly the moment to simply leave altogether, I've got to be thinking about where my next meal will be coming from and this is hardly the season . . ." The key's grooves finally found their matching parts in the lock and it was opened with reluctant creaks. ". . . Ah."

A little bell tinkled satisfyingly as the door eased open and moths lackadaisically flapped into remote recesses, transfiguring into dust or shadows. I turned again to look at her, and she was smiling at me, her face betraying a sweet irony. "Well," she said, "We'll get you all sorted out, Mr. Waiter."

She rummaged cursorily through some drawers at the back of the shop, leaving me to my own devices, which happened to be working at half-speed that particular morning. She soon reappeared with an old-fashioned bow tie in a deep shade of maroon. I stood straight as a pike my heart thumping wildly as she approached wrapping her arms around me, her fingers tickling the back of my neck as she tried to fasten my tie. I found myself starting to feel a bit faint and in order to somehow pull myself together I started talking again.

"My father always used to say, as though he were

reciting something dictated by God himself, that a man oughtn't to think of himself as above his post and while I suppose strictly speaking we don't think of ourselves as having posts anymore generally speaking and moreover I don't think of myself as either above or below waitering *per se* I also don't believe that I want to be my job like my father was the textbook fireman even at home where he would spend his nights off endlessly fireproofing the rooms and conducting patrols for all manner of fire hazard . . ."

I stopped to draw a breath and she suddenly found the clasp, took away her slender arms, and gave me one hand to kiss. "My name is Dalia," she crooned. I brought her hand to my mouth and clumsily kissed it. "Roy," I stammered. "Well, Roy, your fifteen minutes are almost up."

My flush of rapture transformed in an instant to the all-too-familiar cold shiver of sudden horror. Without a word of farewell I threw open the door once again and plunged into the fog-smeared streets.

The day after drew itself out impossibly far, like a cat stretching out after a mid-afternoon nap, threatening to crack in the middle and spill open piñata-like. Was it somehow this quality, looming heavily in the very air, afflicting even the barometrically-precise atmosphere of the Restaurant, that caused my mind to tunnel backwards to a Mexican folk tale I'd read as a child? My thoughts preferring currents of Central American sunshine to the impossible banality of silver polishing?

Padre Paramo was endlessly forgetting his glasses. Like clockwork, he would remember just as he was climbing the small rise of white-washed stone steps leading infallibly to the modest chapel where he presided over twenty-nine people, or sometimes only twelve, depending on the weather. As the padre would step up to the altar the congregation would howl like a chorus of Hallelujahs, "Your glasses, Padre Paramo!" and then cry with laughter as the sheepish man of the cloth would stumble off the altar and back home to get his glasses. Sometimes this would happen more than once in the course of a single morning, as the padre would get back home, enjoy a cup of tea, and be so distracted by some thought or other that he would entirely forget the purpose of his journey home, and return to the chapel bare-faced, to the delight and merriment of the thinning congregation.

It was on one such morning that Pedro Paramo was hurrying to church, his glasses lying mischievously on his bedside table, when he was apprehended by a voice from the side of the road.

"If you can spare a second, Father, I am in need of some holy counsel."

If the padre had been wearing his glasses he would surely have been alarmed by such a request coming from the mouth of a pack mule, in particular a pack mule with crimson flames leaping wildly in his eyes. As it was, the padre could only squint and imagine that some young and bright-eyed lad was standing before him, seeking the guidance of the Lord. Late though he was for his sermon, he was a good-hearted man who could not refuse to perform a service.

"I must travel for many miles today, Father, and have left the house without any kind of relic around my neck to ward off the unholy spirits. Would you be so kind as to lend me a cross for the journey?"

The padre hesitated, for the only cross he had about him was the one that he kept over his heart. "Come with me to the chapel, Son, and I will find you a cross there."

The father resumed walking, but the voice soon stopped him once again. "I have no time to walk the full distance to the chapel Padre Paramo . . . for I must start my travels at once! Surely you could forfeit the crossss around your neck for merely a short time . . ."

The way the stranger drew out the "s" in "cross" and was unaccountably familiar with his Christian name awakened Paramo's sense of caution . . . yet he could not refuse to proffer the strength of the Lord to one in need . . . and so he undid the crucifix and slowly handed it over to the donkey, whose eyes glowed ever more brightly with greed. Just as the poor holy man was about to relinquish the cross, the donkey's hoof pierced the thick fog of his crippled vision, and he recognized it as the hand of the Devil. Padre Paramo drew back and swung the cross into the beast's face, which howled and vanished.

"There you are . . . I've been hunting all over for you!"

Indeed, I had hidden myself in an out-of-the-way corner and begun mutely polishing a hill of lusterless silverware. Alfred chuckled understandingly and sat down beside me to help polish. Alfred was a waiter too. We worked together silently for some time, enjoying the partial oasis of solidarity and calm, before I allowed myself some carefully measured words.

"Say, Alfred . . . Do you like working here? . . . At the Restaurant, I mean . . ."

"Why, sure, Roy . . . I think I like it just fine . . . Yes, just fine indeed."

"But do you not find, Alfred (here a gentle cough) . . . Do you not find, from time to time . . . that one starts to act the part of the waiter even though there is no one, in fact, to be serving?"

"How do you mean, Roy?" asked Alfred somewhat rhetorically, his voice betraying a gentle quavering or perhaps a tremolo effect.

"It can happen in a number of ways, Alfred. Maybe you'll feel a flush of panic when your meal takes more than fifteen minutes to prepare. Maybe you've started putting inedible sprigs of decorative garnish alongside your cutlets. Or perhaps it is merely a vague and ephemeral anxiety that you are forever displeasing a second party in your own house that does . . . not . . . exist."

Plainly I had touched a nerve. Alfred had been jerkily polishing the same salad fork for the whole of the conversation, and all the while was uneasily peering over his shoulder. I pressed on.

"But perhaps the most unsettling part, Alfred, is in what I sense this means. Somehow, deep in the core of your humanity you must feel as though there is some essential truth to *this* (here a dramatic sweep of an arm to indicate the Restaurant), that the simple truth is that there are people born to be served upon, and others born to serve, and that you, Alfred . . . or rather we . . ."

At which point a crash rang out from somewhere in the Restaurant and Alfred, clearly of the belief that any flatware breakage was bound to be a lesser horror than the present conversation, drew himself up and flung himself in the direction of the noise. I resumed my polishing and the rest of the day passed without event.

That night however, I fell under some manner of possession. My thoughts would begin in the most diverse of terrains: Alfred, the stars visible through the window despite the condensation, my father's chronic illness, the restoring warmth from a simple cup of tea, and always, always, navigate a trail back to the ample reservoir of

Dalia: Dalia whose hand I had kissed, Dalia who could smile in twelve ways, Dalia, a cosmos in five letters. Before long I was merely sitting and staring blankly at a wall, whereupon I shook myself and coaxed my body to bed.

The following morning was worse than ever. I could only watch in strangled terror as the Waiter took pains with the table settings and felt a twinge of shame at sitting down to eat breakfast while there was still work waiting to be done. He was revolted by the little red spots on the tablecloth. Tired of the conflict, I left for the Restaurant to give the Waiter his due time.

On the street outside my house I spied the little body of a freshly-killed pigeon on its side. It was in the middle of the street where many more automobiles were likely to run it over before the end of the day. Christian duty seemed to suggest moving the thing over to the side of the road, but dead birds often carry diseases.

As the crafted façade of the Restaurant came into sight, as its shadow came sweeping over me like an evil spirit, I experienced a fearsome shudder run through my very bones. As though dark wings had enveloped my heart, only for one timid moment. I breathed in deeply, checked my pulse, and pushed open the heavy glass doors of the Restaurant.

"The weather's taking a turn for the better," volunteered the head waiter. I nodded enthusiastically and smiled, hoping to make him forget my outrageous despondency and forgetfulness from the day before. It was then that I took off my overcoat and caught my reflection in the tall entryway mirror with starched white shirt and no bow tie.

It was the Waiter that flew into a confused rage. I, on the other hand, preserved a stoic calm and even permitted myself some smug delight at this innocent act of sabotage. I watched smirkingly as the Waiter stammered and spluttered, struggling to rationalize the second absurd act in as many days. The head waiter bellowed with all his might, made gestures of exasperation, but this time I could tell that he was simply helpless to stop his facial gymnastics. So he and I stood patiently by as the Waiter and the Head Waiter did their respective routines, culminating with the Waiter sheepishly returning to the cold morning for bow tie number two.

I gained some satisfaction in feeling the Waiter recede, shrinking back in cowardice into some iron-clad depths of my chest the nearer I got to The Bow Tie Co. I felt my chest swell with pride, my stride widen to that of a conqueror's. Only when I was outside the actual doors did it occur to me that I'd no idea what to say.

I could feel the ghoulish chuckle of the Waiter from somewhere within, mocking and undermining my best efforts. I could feel my resolve wilt, and in a moment of crisis nearly turned around. But even such cowardice was futile: there would be no returning to the Restaurant without a tie. Conjuring up something between a hopeless smile and a grimace of pain, I entered the store.

The little bell tinkled idiotically as I entered. There was my Dalia, compelling proof of objective perfection. I swallowed audibly.

"I've lost my bow tie . . . a second time," I announced, as though it were a matter calling for sober reflection, and indeed we stood gravely regarding one another for a moment, her seated angelically behind the service desk, me framed preposterously by the halo of bow ties decorating the doorway, before she exploded with laughter.

"Again? Oh, dear me, such hard luck . . ." she said with a sweet, although suspecting smile. Had I been too obvious? Of course a second day in a row would arouse her suspicions! I suddenly felt violently ill, acids from my stomach rose up to the back of my throat. She went into the back of the shop and, feeling as though I ought to clear up my embarrassment, I began yelling.

"I know it must seem, well, a little odd . . . A second bow tie! . . . But sometimes a fellow is concentrating so hard on not forgetting something, that paradoxically this is precisely the thing he forgets! Why, yesterday I must have said to myself one hundred times, 'I won't be forgetting my bow tie tomorrow!' and naturally . . ." I was cut short by the sound of things falling in the backroom, and was alarmed at the volume my own voice had reached. The store seemed very quiet in its absence.

She soon reappeared with a bow tie of shimmering gold. I could not help smiling, albeit uneasily, in anticipation of what was to come next . . . how she would throw her arms around my neck as she did the day before, lingeringly fastening the clasp of the tie, our mutual pretext . . . she was almost upon me when the insipid tinkling of the damned bell over the door announced an interloper, crushing my beautiful reverie like an eggshell.

If you have been conscientiously following the train of the narrative thus far, perhaps inelegantly executed, but carrying, you must admit, a certain puissance, you will no doubt share to some degree the anguish I felt upon hearing that bell, that knell to sweet amour! But infinitely worse was the sequel. Can one even hope to describe the loathing that infested my heart when Alfred stepped through that door?

Our eyes met for an instant, and immeasurable misery and resignation were mutually communicated. But then I was hit by a flash of anger and I turned again to face Dalia. She was a trifle shaken, and her face had flushed scarlet, but she soon regained her composure, and came to put the bow tie around my collar. What had the day before been such exhilaration, a confirmation of life itself, seemed now infinitely cheapened, degraded, sold at a bargain to a company of phantoms. I knew that

Dalia could sense my despair, her eyes grew sad, but then they twinkled impishly as she put a folded piece of paper into my shirt pocket so cleverly that Alfred couldn't have noticed. Then she coyly took my money and I brushed past Alfred and onto the street. No sooner had the door swung shut behind me than I feverishly unwrapped the note. I have repeated those eight words to myself like a mantra ever since, eight words ascending to the rare summit of joy: "It is only you I love, Mr. Waiter."

I read it five or six times to convince myself that I had not fallen victim to some cruel hallucination or play of the light. Mercifully, I had read it correctly. How my heart kicked from within my poor chest! But I still needed to lay my doubts to rest. With the cuff of my sleeve I wiped a little peephole in the condensation that had formed on the window, so that I might observe Alfred and Dalia together. Her movements with him were objectively similar to how she was with me, yet I noted (and not without satisfaction) that she moved mechanically, almost somnambulently with Alfred. The deep baritone of a church bell trailed me as I floated along the road back to the Restaurant.

Upon arrival, Padre Paramo loudly and passionately delivered a sermon to the assembled parish on the trickery of Satan. He concluded his speech by telling the churchgoers about what had just transpired, that he had nearly been taken in by Satan in the form of a pack mule. The parishioners knew that Padre Paramo would not consciously tell a lie, but then they also understood that he was now an old man, and that each day his brain was growing ever more feeble. So they all indulged him, but when they went home they all joked about the wrath of the demon mule, staging mock dramas of the incident to general amusement.

The padre, oblivious as always, started the long and lonely walk that took him home, still in his short-sighted condition. Soon the clippity-clop of a hooved animal pulling a vehicle was heard behind him. Without his glasses, how could the padre be blamed for failing to notice the flaming eyes of the mule? Or the fleshless terror of the skeleton holding the reins? The covered wagon drew up near and addressed him.

"Padre Paramo, it is a long and dusty road back to your house and I have the good fortune to be traveling in the same direction. Will you do me the service of allowing me to carry you to your home?"

As it spoke, the skeleton's dry fingers drew back the black curtain that obscured the interior of the wagon. Plumes of thick dust flew with the movement of the curtain, causing the padre to sneeze convulsively. He was about to climb in when the skeleton stopped him with a request.

"Oh good Padre, I have forgotten my cross at the last tavern, and have miles upon miles of arduous galloping ahead! Perhaps you might loan me your cross in exchange for the ride?"

Oh, if only I had been about to remind Padre Paramo of his earlier and certainly analogous encounter! If only I could courier my cries of alarm to the ears of the remote padre! But alas, the Devil had not forgotten his previous oversight, and as he stretched forth his skeletal claw to take the cross from our befuddled holy man, he changed it for an instant into the hand of a normal man. Thus the padre forfeited his last hope for salvation and slipped into the shadowy compartment at the rear of the wagon, the curtain falling silently behind him. At once the skeleton tossed away the cross, and the carriage lurched forward at a terrible speed. In the total blackness of the compartment, the padre's head began to fill up with nightmares, coating the inside of his skull like a syrup, whereupon the coach seemed to change direction and began speeding downwards, into the very earth. He stuck a hand out of the curtains, but drew it back immediately, for it had been stung by an icy chill.

At this point in the story I was bringing three bowls of steaming hot minestrone to a table and I nearly dropped them on the pate of a balding gentleman's head, when it occurred to me what had been happening in the story. One thing was certain: in the version I had been told the padre did not start to descend into the foul catacombs of Hell . . . and events in these folk tales invariably happened in threes, whereas Padre Paramo had only encountered the Devil twice before being whisked off. I forced the story out of my mind in order to concentrate on my work. God knows who I had been serving while I was thinking about the story.

It hardly seems worth mentioning that relations between Alfred and myself were a bit strained for the remainder of that day. I knew that Dalia loved me first and foremost, yet somehow Alfred's comical delusions unsettled me. I watched his ostrich-like strutting, his deft showmanship as he weaved amongst the tables, and I longed to show him my note. But I did not.

On the way home, my gaze alighted on that repulsive pigeon once again. It had been utterly flattened during the day's flow of traffic, more of a feathery carpet than a body. My nerves were slightly affected by this, and I vowed to myself to take a different route to work the next day.

That night, sitting lethargically in the center of my soberly decorated kitchen (I rarely permit myself excesses), my imagination ceaselessly orbited around the petty though rich satisfaction of showing Alfred the note I had been given. He would be cockily whistling an insipid melody through his widely-gapped teeth, and here's where I would stroll forward and with a sympathetic but firm pat on the shoulder present the little slip of paper. Or perhaps first I would solicit his opinion, quite innocently, on the matter of the woman we had both encountered at The Bow Tie Co., and once he had gone to great lengths and employed all manner of superlative in describing her finer qualities I would cough lightly and hold the note under his vast aquiline nose. And so I busied myself until I needed to sleep.

The following morning, all was not right in the head. It seemed intact and apart from a blotchy reddening of the eyes altogether physically familiar . . . yet bizarre and often contradictory thoughts swam through it at a terrifying pace. Though my stomach wanted food, I chose to forego breakfast and the tangled confusion that came with it. It seemed I could rest my mind on only one thought . . . that I would purposefully forget my bow tie at home a final time, to exclaim once and for all to Dalia, "I . . . am not a waiter!" This sentence glistened graillike amidst the hopeless morass of my thoughts.

Outside, the streets were a mess. Cars whistling and scampering everywhere, like rodents! I even found myself taking a bit of comfort in the bird-corpse, which remained constant, shiftless, though gradually decomposing into cigarette ends and tattered newspapers which seemed to stick to the soles of my boots before flapping off on a westerly wind. The blinking and monstrous eye of a traffic signal pulsed and echoed in the back of my mind. I struggled to hear vague and muffled whisperings, but in vain. I bellowed at a cloud.

I cannot be sure of this, but my recollection tells me that skeletal footprints marked a path for me in the freshly fallen snow, all the way up to the doors of the Restaurant.

At the threshold, the uproar was deafening. I cradled my head in my hands for a moment or two, snowflakes all the while gently dappling my shoulders. From within the Restaurant walls, sirens and shrieks were wantonly spilling forth, punctuated by that damned blinking light. With a mighty effort I threw my limp body through the doors.

Inside, a delicate Strauss waltz floated demurely over the heads of waiters and bus boys rehearsing their roles. The anguished expression on my face washed itself away. I was about to make a general announcement that I had forgotten my bow tie, and then at the final moment I recalled that I had better keep up appearances. Therefore I pretended to be getting ready for work. I could see the Head Waiter already beginning to study me, peering circumspectly at my neck, which was still obscured by my overcoat. Trembling despite myself under the weight of his leaden gaze, I started unbuttoning my coat, my hands working with excruciating slowness. At last the coat came undone, and I stood defiantly before the Head Waiter, my throat naked as the day I was born. He stared at me in disbelief, and I cringingly sunk my hands into the depths of my pockets. In one I felt an alien lump. I pulled it out in surprise, and when I saw what I had in my hand, the blood drained from my face.

It was my bow tie. But who had put it into my pocket? I searched inside of myself to find the Waiter, to drag him out and demand an explanation, but he was cowering somewhere cavernous and shady. The Head Waiter saw my bow tie and my confusion and a thin smile disfigured his lips. Orange flames pranced in his eyes. I fell into a dead faint.

I was brought back to life by a bowl of warm soup and some soothing aphorisms from a cook. I picked myself up and put in a full day of work. The day was fine, but the odd thing was . . . that I could no longer tell if I was myself or the Waiter . . . or both, or neither. The only thing I could be certain of was that the conflict had been resolved. And Dalia, dear, dear, Dalia, had all the pain, nostalgia and remoteness of a faded photograph.

Now from time to time I catch my hand absent-mindedly composing a love letter to you, Dalia, perhaps on the backside of a torn cocktail napkin or the bill for a meal I have cleared off a table. In the confusion that ensues when it occurs to me what I have been doing, I normally crumple it up and throw it in a wastebin. But sometimes, without any certainty as to what for, I will fold it up and carry it with me in a shirt-pocket.

THE CELLAR

If it did not sound nonsensical, I should say that it was nothing and yet something, or that it was and yet was not. Whatever it is, it must have been there first, able to be the vehicle for all the composite forms which we can see in the world.

Saint Augustine, *Confessions*

Let us suppose that our narrator whom we have been accompanying thus far is suddenly revealed to be a university professor. How does this alter our understanding of the story? And if he is an ex-convict? A Catholic? A misanthrope? It is my intention to prove that these, shall we say, gaps, sometimes unintentionally filled in by the reader, do not exist until they are revealed to exist. Furthermore, information that is candidly supplied can at times contradict the implied story, or the actual narrative. This "actual narrative" belongs wholly to the reader and is all that can be said to exist of the narrative proper. The role of the narrator, then, is to provide as little interference as possible with the greatest number of actual narratives. For example.

I had finally found the address among the piles of papers which never seemed more futile than when I was searching for something among them . . . "I'll throw them all out tomorrow," I vowed to myself, and then to the papers, "Your days are numbered!" Do I need to confirm . . . have you already suspected . . . that all of the papers were in the same handwriting? The corners all bent due to the same nervous habit, a tic or twitch?

I folded the address twice in half and then slipped it into my back pocket. The sun was setting more quickly than usual, and I wasn't certain where I was headed (the address was in an unfamiliar part of town), but it seemed to me that I would need half an hour to get there. I set out westerly, having to avert my eyes from the unpleasantry of the sun at the horizon. Every time I thought to look, the silhouettes of a dozen or so birds were being tossed to and fro by a wind said to be coming from the mountains.

How long had I been walking before I saw that I was being followed? Between five and seven minutes. What was my most immediate reaction? A quickening of the heart, an attempt to maintain a natural composition of the face and gait. The latter belonging to the voluntary class of movements. Describe the figure appearing to be in pursuit. Rather too shadowy to provide a suitable description, but wearing heavy-soled shoes which made a clattering sound whenever he scurried out of sight, into an alcove of this or that building.

I should mention that my nerves had already been adversely affected by the goings-on in my apartment building. I had originally lived on the fourth floor, and indeed resided there in some comfort for a number of years. But then about four months ago I had started to sense the chill. At first I had taken it to be a strangely persistent draft, not at all an unreasonable hypothesis for late November. And so I took to double-sealing the windows, stuffing old sweaters into the cracks under the doors, taping plastic bags over the ventilation openings. Yet somehow the chill always persisted, as though seeping in from all directions, as though somehow the walls themselves were cold. For a time I tried to be indifferent to it, but I found that I could not shake the sensation that the chill was slowly penetrating the outer layers of my skin, leaving a dead epidermic shell, and gradually breaching the tegument altogether and occupying the flesh, the bones, moving in to conquer the heart. A week later I had moved to a nearly identical apartment on the seventh floor.

You can imagine my horror, then, to find that the chill in the new apartment was even more intense than that of the previous. This cold came to occupy my thoughts at all times, everything I did was painted in frosty blue or damp gray. My friends tired of hearing me talk about the problem and so I was compelled to stop mentioning it, for fear that they would start to think me obsessive or mad. Then I was quite literally alone with the bestial cold, and it was all I could do to move a third time, now to the sixteenth and uppermost floor.

When I truly understood the depths of the all-piercing numbness that fell upon me in that sixteenth-floor apartment, I came to long for the merely unsettling chill of the fourth floor. This newest cold affected me at very nearly every level of my emotional and physical being. And when I finally entered the relative solace of a chattering sleep, it pursued me in my dreams, whether personified as a spectral, bone-white child, dressed in silks, with patches of hair missing, or simply felt as a lurking presence behind whatever improbable dream façade I had thrown up. But I say "very nearly" every level, for there was somewhere a part of my mind that was yet mercifully unaffected, fiddling at the miniature Pompei-effect that was consuming the remainder of my body.

And I now know that the part which categorically refused to relent was the actual source of the suffering, and not the chill itself, for without it I would have had nothing to contrast with. Therefore, to soothe my one percent I took to frequent strolling, and delighted in the temporary thawing of the tips of my digits in the paper-thin air of the False Spring.

It was on one of these strolls along boulevards built in gentler eras that I hit upon the solution to my problem. It had such a natural, crystalline ring of truth to it that I could not believe that I hadn't come up with it sooner. I had been moving higher, ever higher in the building, and accordingly the chill had intensified. Therefore, it stood to provisional reason that on the first floor the chill would be at its least powerful, and altogether negated in the cellar. My head swam at the elegant simplicity of my solution. I began smiling, and even tipped my hat to an attractive woman, who merely blushed in response.

Yet a tangle persisted.

An old man was living alone in the only cellar apartment, an unsightly one-room box with pipes erupting out of the walls and a vague moldering smell, the elusive source of which the building superintendent had been trying to locate for years. The aesthetic shortcomings of the place amounted to disagreeable trifles, but of more serious and immediate concern was the old man. He had been living in the place for almost thirty-seven years and harbored a resolute determination to die in the room where he had waited out with equal stubbornness the latter installment of his life's chronicle.

Despite this setback, I felt certain that my obstinacy at that juncture could find no parallel. Even on my four-times-daily walks, my mind's confabulations scarcely wandered from the riddle of how to separate the old man from his suite. My conclusion, again, had a certain simplicity to it; first, I would try to bribe him. Failing that, I would do my best to trick him. Only as a final resort would I kill him.

I am concerned that eyes thoughtlessly scanning these pages for the gist may grow wide in moral indignation and startled wonderment at my final solution. The moistened fingers turning each page at the upper-right-hand corner may blanch at my jarringly inappropriate suggestion. And when it is all laid out on paper like this, in the coarse and one-dimensional fabric of this smudgy ink, I have to agree that my decision appears oddly impulsive, unwarranted even. But if I only had some way of transporting you to the arctic agony of that sixteenth-floor apartment! Even if only for a minute.

The old man's name, I found out, was W. Whittman, just like that of the great American marketing analyst. He made it a rule to never leave the house before two o'clock each afternoon. And so I carried all the money I could raise at such short notice in a brown paper bag at noon one day down the seventeen flights of stairs and knocked confidently on Mr. Whittman's door. For about five minutes nobody answered, but I knew he was there from the audible shuffling and snorting noises that came from within. Finally the door came open, only by a crack.

How was the old man dressed? Shabbily. Various

shades of green and brown. Checkered pants tailored according to the fashion criteria of a long-forgotten era. Wire-rimmed glasses. How was I regarded through the slightly-open door? With extreme caution, but not without a certain curiosity he was helpless to conceal. How did I respond in my anxiety and impatience? I wiped my hands against the legs of my trousers, glanced once or twice over my shoulder, as though expecting to see the shiny boots of the law descending the stairs.

"I live upstairs" I said, and suddenly feeling this explanation to be woefully inadequate added hastily, "On the sixteenth floor."

He stared at me for a minute or two, and I felt my anxiety soaring and swelling inside, billowing out like a sail. At last a limp smile drew his lips back onto the rims of his teeth. "Why don't you step inside?" I heard him graciously offer, though his mouth didn't seem to budge, and I followed him into the apartment.

"Well, it was kind of you to drop by and talk to an old man" was the next thing I heard, and a surprisingly strong hand was guiding me out the door. With a jolt I realized that somehow my visit with the old man was ending, and in my surprise all I could do was sheepishly wave good-bye. And then the door was shut.

Whereupon I stood in the corridor trying to calmly assess what had gone on in the old man's room. I consulted my watch and saw that twenty minutes had elapsed since I stumbled in through the door. A quick rummage through my pockets revealed that my money had been taken, all of it. Had I successfully bribed him with it then? My suspicions veered towards the negative. Was my body in any way injured? A cursory examination revealed no visible markings. What had transpired during that twenty-minute period? I had three hypotheses. One: my feverish state prior to the encounter combined with the fluctuating temperature of my body had me in a state of shock, resulting in a temporary paralysis of the part of the brain responsible for short-term memory. Two: I hit my head on something while entering the room, and when the old man noticed that I was reviving he guided me out of his room. Three: the old man is schooled in some form of hypnosis or mind control, and had me under a trance from the moment I stepped into his room.

On any other day, none of these answers would have struck me as reasonable or satisfactory. On any other day, I might have snickered at my own powers of deduction and discarded all three theories in favor of a sober discussion with the old man. "Look here" I'd have said on this hypothetical infinitude of days, "I've just had a confusing experience, let's see if we can't sort out together what happened." With my sleeve I would have wiped the layer of dust from the top of this so-called mystery, this half-baked enigma, cleared away this poor man's Sphinx and shone the light of pure reason on the subject. Which is to say, on any other day I would not have gone thundering up the seventeen flights of stairs in order to collect my carving knife.

And Lord only knows what might have happened if I had not been utterly winded and my rage replaced with concern for the welfare of my poor, overtaxed heart after maybe eleven or twelve flights. And there I stood for a time, in the austere stairwell, clutching at my chest with a claw-like hand. And when I did make it up to the sub-arctic horror of my home, I was an altogether more rational fellow. Give it a week, I thought, and maybe things will clear up on their own.

On the contrary, things appeared to grow ever more obscure. There was a total lack of contact with the old man, and I came to understand that he was waiting for me to make the next move. Possibly plotting some further deceptions. Every decision I arrived at seemed deeply flawed.

Why did I start writing letters? To mail them, simply, to lend my stride the authentic motivation of a man with a destination. To ward off the numbness in my fingers while at home through the act of writing. Why did I mail them all to myself? For I had to mail them somewhere. Illuminate the purpose of keeping them all in piles on the kitchen table. I plead guilty to a certain fascination with the process my mind was undergoing, observable through a chronological reading of my own letters. And so I read my mail to myself, then? Yes, regularly. And did any of the contents surprise me? On occasion I was even shocked by what I found on those sheaves. Characterize the contents. Unpredictable, written as though by two or more people, and each of them at least mildly schizophrenic. There are disagreements, misunderstandings, interrogations. Nothing is conclusive.

In those days how I yearned for the cellar! Anyone who has ever endured sleepless nights with the thought of a faraway lover, hovering apparition-like and just out of clutching distance and the alarm clock clacking arrhythmically might . . . but no, nonsense, that is an entirely different matter! My appetite waned, my face was covered in painful wounds from having shaved with trembling hands. The cellar was recast as a fantasy kingdom, unmarred by the ravages of civilization. Lilacs sprouted through the cracks in the floor, Wagner was piped in through the ventilation shafts, weren't there swans in the bathtub?

It was a Friday afternoon, then, and I was standing with my nose pressed up against the glass of a window, the distant avenues taking off in all directions, but one and all decisively blocked by the impasse of the horizon. Cars glided to and fro. The display made me chuckle absentmindedly.

I first recognized that something was wrong when it

seemed as though a tremor was destroying the streets below. I staggered back in surprise, but it wasn't the street, it was my head reeling. I sat down heavily, pouring myself a glass of gin. Shortly the spins de-intensified and I was able to think with some lucidity . . . and a single thought occupied my mind.

I am inclined to believe that there is no such thing, really, as a premeditated murder. A murder suggests itself, then the idea is discarded, the thought is resurrected a few times at the most inopportune moments, and not evaluated very carefully. And then one day, you are all of a sudden caught in a moment of weakness, and then you don't stop to plan at all, it's just as though you're being whisked along on a blustery wind or perhaps a merry-go-round (albeit on a coal-black horse).

Finally, then, I really went to the upper drawer and pulled out the carving knife, started to sharpen it, but then taken aback by my own ghoulishness deftly slipped the blade up the length of my sleeve.

I jogged slowly down the seventeen flights of stairs as though trying to give myself time to talk myself out of it, my hands turning black from sliding down the ash-covered rails. In the cellar I began to entertain certain doubts. Too late, too late. I had descended the full distance, my arm stiff as a board to conceal the blade of the knife. No, there would be no turning back.

Describe my emotional state. Scattered, delirious,

all-consuming anxiety. Any physical evidence of this fear (irregular rhythm of the heart, shortness of breath, awareness of noises that in fact did not exist, etc.)? My ears felt burning hot . . . I kept hearing what I thought was my pulse. At what time did I run bursting into the old man's room? By my watch it was 16:27.

At precisely the stroke of 16:47 I was staggering out of the old man's room, knife in hand and pulling the door shut behind me. My arms and neck were covered in blood. And my mind was a monochrome of gray, when I tried to remember the previous twenty minutes, flimsy shadows of memories emerged for a moment and then dispersed like plumes of smoke. I could not even recall if the old man was dead! Sense was awakening in my mind with the new eclipse of panic. I could not be cornered in the macabre blind alley of the cellar, covered in blood, and holding a sharp weapon. I tore off, taking care not to bloody the walls with my hands.

At the fourth floor I stopped dead. Voices and footsteps, stampeding down the stairwell. For a dreadful second I imagined that I was trapped in between floors, up was disastrous and back down unthinkable . . . but then to my fathomless relief I thought of ducking onto the fourth-floor landing. As my hands were, you recall, smeared with blood, I had the good sense to open the door with my teeth, which had never been so dexterous as they were at that second. I squeezed through the door and pressed my ear against it to bear witness to the following.

"When the materials are all prepared and ready, the architects shall appear, I swear to you . . . ," came the round and soothing baritone from behind the door," . . . they shall appear without fail, I swear to you they will understand you . . ."

Back in my apartment, I set about trying to wash away the blood. If you have ever tried to wash the blood from a wound with nothing but water drawn from frozen pipes, you will know that the sediment can be cleaned away, but the skin will somehow remain dyed a ghastly rosé, exactly as though I'd just been born. As for my shirt, I threw it with revulsion into the bathtub, not wanting to have to look at the loathsome thing. It lay curled up and exhausted like an old dog. My apartment felt impossibly small, built for someone half my height. I needed to go for a walk, but felt that an alibi was necessary. Who could say when the bloodhounds might turn up. I recalled that in one of my letters to myself I had scribbled an address. Characterize the handwriting. Heavily slanted backwards as though swept by some persistent draft, evidence in places of unsteadiness of hand, where one might presume the writer experienced an attack of the nerves. Large loops for the tops of the "h's," and the bottoms of the "g's." The writer? Well, that is to say, I.

All of which guides us by the scarlet hand to the street, from before the start of the recollection, drops us back onto that streetcorner, pursued by a cindery shadow that is coming more and more to resemble the old man who lived or lives in the cellar. The silhouettes of those birds haven't budged, they might be stitched onto the sunset but for the skipping effect which makes them shudder for an instant before resettling in their places. My body pleads exhaustion with the rhetoric of a trained salesman.

Why did I bend over? To pick up an address that had fallen out of my back pocket and fluttered moth-like to the pavement. What suddenly caught my eye as I paused, stooped over? A gentle layering effect, for I was already standing in the shadow of a towering building when a massive truck pulled up, drowning me in a second coat of shadow, pulling another ephemeral curtain between the sun and I. As I was straightening up, what drew my attention?

The figure now just a few feet away, apparently waiting for me to get up. Such was the intensity of the sunset behind him that I could make out none of the specifics of his features, but I was somehow confident that he was smiling. He lowered his inky hand down to reach mine, to pull me up, all the while mumbling in that same soothing and low drawl, "That thou O God my life has lighted, with ray of light . . ." A warm rush like a gulp of whiskey or the ease of amnesia swept through my weary limbs, ". . . my latest word, here on my knees, old, poor, and paralyzed I yield my ships to Thee . . ."

Well, wouldn't you know it. After that encounter I went home entirely new. I opened the door to my top-floor apartment and a blast of warm air smacked me in the face. Just like that! Golden rays of twinkling sun tore through the windows with such dramatic force that I had to squint. As though the garden walls had crumbled and Spring were allowed to arrive. And then what did I care for the cellar, entangled in rusty pipes, under countless layers of dust and decay? A fanciful birdsong twittered monotonously just outside my window, repeating itself as though mechanized. The shirt I had thrown in the tub had crawled off, leaving only crimson paw prints in its wake.

A long and weary sigh arose in my chest. What did it indicate to me? I shuffled to the liquor cabinet and poured myself a tumbler of vodka. What did the sigh indicate? I took modest sips, reacquainting myself with the slow burn of the throat. The sigh? I fell into a chair, watching the first traces of night smooth out the imper-fections of the day, the day, the day seeping like blood through the cracks in one hundred sidewalks.

Soren Alberto Gauger was born in Nova Scotia, Canada in 1975 and took a degree in literature from Simon Fraser University in Vancouver. Having held various jobs — actor, musician, flower deliveryman, waiter — he now lives in Kraków, Poland where he has worked as a writer, translator, and literature professor-at-large at Jagiellonian University. His work has appeared in a number of publications in the U.S. and Canada, including a chapbook entitled *Quatre Regards sur l'Enfant Jesus* (Ravenna Press, 2004). He is currently translating a volume of short stories by the Polish writer Jerzy Ficowski.

HYMNS TO MILLIONAIRES by Soren A. Gauger is a first
edition published in 2004 by TWISTED SPOON PRESS
P.O. Box 21 – Preslova 12, 150 21 Prague 5, Czech
Republic, www.twistedspoon.com • cover and frontispiece
engravings by Cristian Opriş • photograph of author by
Tomasz Zugaj • text set in New Baskerville • designed by J.
Slast • printed in the Czech Republic by Akcent, Vimperk •
grateful acknowledgment is made to the editors of the
following publications where some of the stories in this
volume have previously appeared: *The Capilano Review*;
Jacob's Ladder #2; *Milk Magazine*; *Prague Literary Review*;
Snow Monkey; *Spork* • the author would like to thank Marcin,
Paweł, Raf, Saygun, Cristian, Kuba, and family in its broadest
definition • available to the trade in North America by
SCB DISTRIBUTORS: 15608 South New Century Drive,
Gardena, CA 90248

1-800-729-6423 / www.scbdistributors.com

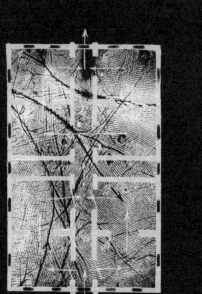